GW01018551

WHISKEY

GIRL

Copyright 2018 by Adriane Leigh

Editing: Silently Correcting Your Grammar
Photographer: Wander Aguir
Model: Victorio Piva
Beta Reader: Karen Lawson

Printed in the U.S.A.

FIRST EDITION

WHISKEY

GIRL

ADRIANE LEIGH

*She was the one thing holding him together. Until
she was gone.
And then there was whiskey.*

*Fallon Gentry has spent the last decade reliving one
dark night in his head. The moment he lost the woman he
loved when a single blink cascaded into a series of
events that stole both of their lives. Now his nights are
spent playing music in southern honky-tonks and nursing
the memory of her the only way he knows how—at the
bottom of a whiskey bottle.*

*A brief stint in Nashville, a hit song, and a brush
with Hollywood couldn't bring him closer to God, but
when the ghost of Augusta Belle Branson appears in his
corner of another lonely dive bar well after dark, he's
forced to confront everything he thought he knew about
that fateful night…and a few things he didn't.*

He's her contradiction. She's his salvation.

*A firestorm of emotion consumes them when they
come together after ten lost years, every moment more
revealing, more unpredictable, more intoxicating than
the next. Until the only reckoning left for Fallon is the
one he must make with himself. But this time, fate may
have left an afterburn too bitter to swallow. This time, he
may lose his whiskey girl for good.*

Dearest Reader & Rebel Heart,

There are exactly three sex scenes in this book.

THREE out of more than FIFTY.

I say this because many of you, my gorgeous book babes, are used to reading Adriane Leigh (and Aria Cole) books that are brimming with glorious and gratuitous sexytimes.

I love those books.

They're as much a part of me as this one.

But this one isn't those.

My hope is you'll spend the next 300 pages so consumed by the raw, complicated, messy beauty that is Fallon and Augusta's love that you won't even notice the difference.

Or maybe you will.

This book isn't different for me because there's less sexy, (although I would totally argue that this slow-burn thing they have going is even MORE SEXY!) it's different in ALL the ways for me.

Because you, book babes, are my tribe, I feel compelled to tell you that it's been a wild, life-changing journey in the nearly six years I've been publishing, but it's been a whirlwind in just the last six months.

Truly.

Firstly…

White Heat.

It's been written for two years. I have only to finish the edits, completely rewrite the ending because, guys, I'm a totally different writer now than I was two years ago (shocker, right?) and hopefully get it released by the end of 2018.

White Heat was the book I sat down to edit in April.

Instead, Whiskey Girl happened.

Rewind to all the years of unhealthy habits leaving me worn-out and feeling more under pressure than ever. I had to trim my life to the bare bones and introduce some better habits, or I would continue to live in the negative headspace and spiral of anxiety and guilt. Wife. Mother. Daughter. Friend. Reader. Woman. Traveler. Writer. Where was I in all of this?

I had to give myself a minute.

Like a time-out. With wine.

The one thing I knew for sure was that I needed to write more stories that fed my soul. Writing has been my passion for as long as I've been reading, I knew that, whatever else I did, I'd need to write more. A lot more. Books that challenged me in new ways, stories that spoke to me on levels I didn't even understand.

I'd already started the habit of daily yoga and meditation, and one lesson out of so many that it's taught me is the practice of giving myself grace.

No more striving to be the best. I'm only striving to be the best me.

So come April, I was primed and ready.

I wrote the majority of Whiskey Girl in three weeks around my 35th birthday. First at 2,500 word-a-day sprints, and then 4,000 words a day when the story really got cookin'! I couldn't stop!

So why do I tell you this?

Because I think of you each like my girlfriends, and I felt like I had some 'splainin' to do! It's taken me a longgg damn time to find out who I am. Down on the way deep inside, not my mother's voice criticizing every detail, my own self-fulfilling prophecies looking to confirm the sense of unworthiness and failure. It took me a minute to learn that voice is bullshit. A stone-cold LIAR!

What matters is doing the work in front of me, connecting to the passion and serious creative flow of the universe as I do it. Those two things come together, and magic happens.

It took me more than TWO YEARS to release a book! Thank you for hanging in there, I couldn't even attempt to write a sentence without your love, support, cheerleading, smiles, funny gifs, and inspiring photography (wink).

I love you each, more than I thought my heart could hold.

And finally, I don't know about anyone else, but the Royal Wedding is still giving me life. SO MUCH INSPIRATION!

If you like overly styled amateur photos, I'd love to connect with more of you on the 'Gram! When I'm not writing or reading books, I'm taking pictures of them like an epic nerd and living the good life on Instagram under adriane.leigh.writer!

And if you're really feeling the love and want to get alllll the book news before anyone else, search "Adriane's Rebel Hearts" on Facebook to join my reader group. Drop in, grab a book, share a story, we'd love to have you!

Before my rambling gets away from me (that's what Instagram is for, y'all), thank you for being a part of my #goodvibetribe.

You're the best.

The cream of the crop.

Top-shelf, all the way.

This book is for you.

I hope you love it as much as Fallon loves his whiskey girl.

xo Adriane

ONE

Fallon

The first time I met Augusta Belle Branson, she was fixin' on killin' herself.

Said the minute I'd walked up, she was tryin' to decide if jumpin' off the bridge in the center—where the water was deep and the current stronger—would be a swifter end, or if she should jump near the edge, where jagged limestone slabs anchored the slow-moving current.

Certain death for sure.

I replayed the split second when the Indian summer sun burst through the orange oak leaves, a halo of warmth enveloping her.

Like an angel. Stardust sparkling straight from heaven, ploppin' her in my path.

And then she turned, the most startling shade of

liquid amber eyes breathing something real and alive, like fire, into my soul.

That same something I'd been runnin' from—*or chasin'*, dependin' on how you looked at it—just about every day since.

I settled myself on the lone wooden stool that awaited at center stage, my thoughts drawing back to the present. My head swam, but the old familiar chords floated on through the current of whiskey in my blood, and I strummed the first few notes of a song I wrote a lot of nights ago by an act of sheer muscle memory.

Old acoustic guitar resting on my knee, my first and third fingers in position on the strings, the opening chords of "Whiskey Girl" bled from my fingers.

Every chord, another dagger.

Every whispered lyric, my undoing.

I still 'didn't know what the fuck had overtaken me the night I'd written this song in a fevered rush.

Well, the booze might have played a part, but I happened to think my best shit came out of uninhibited states.

I'd just had a fuckton of uninhibited states recently.

And the harder the liquor, the more she haunted me.

Whiskey Girl.

My poisoned lullaby.

The crowd of a few hundred erupted into a standing ovation when I ended with the final, emotion-charged words.

The irony of this song was it was the one that'd launched my career. The first single to hit radio waves and then the top spot on the Billboard charts, and brought reporters, music executives, long-lost family members I wasn't even really sure I was related to, and too much other scum with an end game that carried dollar signs to my front doorstep.

I'd moved to Nashville a rising star and left two years later, middle finger in the air as I tossed my once-promising music career out with last night's liquor bottles in favor of the open road.

Chasing something.

Not finding the one thing I needed.

Playing local honky-tonks for a fraction of the money I could have made.

But the truth was, the road was the only place I could find my happy.

A familiar ball of pain formed in my throat as I stood, pushing my guitar over one shoulder and bowing deeply. I couldn't see a single face behind the glaring stage lights, but still, some part of me pretended she could be out there, that I was singing to her.

That she would hear her song and find her way back to me.

After hundreds of faceless crowds and too many bottles of Tennessee whiskey to bother counting, I still felt the pull inside me to travel to every town in America if that's what it took to find her.

Hell, maybe she was happily married with a few kids, a dog, and a fucking minivan by now.

I nodded my head, giving one last wave to the crowd in the dark beyond, then left the stage, taking the steps two at a time and angling past the curtains to head for the tiny-ass dressing room this dive bar provided. Heading for another chug of amber gold before packing my shit into my truck and hitting the road.

I pushed a hand through my hair, thinking maybe a shower would be in order before I bailed, when a curvy little thing backed right up into me.

My palms landed on her shoulders, warm blond waves falling in a cascade over one side. The heady scent of peaches and honey filled my nostrils. My eyes slammed closed and brought me back to summer nights under a giant oak, fireflies melding together with the stars above like a painting.

"Sorry, I just dropped my phone." The sweet-scented creature spun, brilliant smile falling from her face when our eyes made contact for the first time.

Every coldhearted memory slammed into my chest like a pallet of bricks.

I narrowed my eyes, gaze tracing the familiar yet unfamiliar angles of her porcelain face.

She was thinner now, cheeks sharp slashes of bone

that highlighted her always-devastating round eyes and full lips. It was her, all right. I'd know this woman anywhere.

"Hi, Fallon." I'd been dreamin' of this moment for the better part of a decade, and still, my heart wasn't prepared for those two words. My name on her lips left me with a toxic reaction.

My whiskey girl.

My damnation and my salvation.

"I need a fucking minute." I dropped my hands from her shoulders, her skin still haunting my fingertips, and walked straight down the narrow hallway, pushing the rusted back door open so hard the hinges protested.

Warm night air filled my lungs, replacing the empty feeling seeing her again had left.

"Fallon…" Hell, she'd followed me out.

And hell if wanted her to, but I didn't *not* want her to either.

The emotions bombarding my mind were just a-fucking-bout unbearable.

"I said I *need* a fucking minute." The sentence came out as more of a growl than I intended. Before she could reply, I stomped across the potholed parking lot, aiming for my heavy-duty Ford.

I yanked the door open, digging behind the driver's seat for a fresh bottle of my favorite recipe.

I couldn't be bothered to retrieve the half-full bottle I'd

left in my dressing room. I had to get as far the fuck away from her just to clear my head and process what her being here even meant.

My hands circled the neck of the bottle, and I opened it in a flash, chugging back the first warm bite of pleasure I'd been craving.

I tossed the cap on my dash and fished the keys out of my pocket, about to climb into the cab and make hay, when fingertips painted a dark navy filtered into my vision and back out again, my goddamn truck keys hanging from one finger.

"Fuck," I bit out, crawling out of the cab and swiping for the keys.

My reactions were a helluva lot slower than I thought they were. *How much of that bottle had I drunk before the show?* I shook the thought from my head, realizing this was probably about close to my average state of play on any given day. Runnin' away from the life Augusta Belle and I'd had took something out of me. Something only whiskey could fill.

"I don't care what your stupid ass does on your own time, but you're not dying on mine, Fallon Gentry."

My head pounded then. A whole fucking sentence out of her pretty pink lips, and my body's old dependable reaction to her infuriating every cell of me.

I'd never been in control when it came to Augusta. Shouldn't have been surprised it was no different now.

"As irritating as ever, I see," I said, swiping for my keys one more time and missing before I stumbled off around her, whiskey bottle clutched in my hand and hell on my mind.

Augusta was back, and there wasn't enough whiskey in the state of Tennessee to help me deal.

TWO

Fallon

A pile driver found its way inside my chest, cleaving my heart in fucking two as I walked out of the dusty parking lot, eyes lost in the darkness far out ahead of me. The girl of my dreams waitin' next to my truck behind me.

I slugged another mouthful of the hot whiskey, the fire burnin' down my throat and leavin' a trail of raw fucking pain, just like Augusta Belle had done.

Where in the fuck had she been?

My brain tried to wrap itself around the pain of her leavin', her comin' back, fucking with my life in ways I didn't understand.

I kicked at a rock, watching it tumble over the gray asphalt before I veered left, deciding I wanted to be off this road if Augusta Belle took a mind to hop into my truck and chase me down. I didn't really care if she drove it, though I'd never let anyone else, but the idea of her sittin' behind that big wheel made a half smile turn my lips.

Augusta Belle Branson was back, after all these years. I'll be damned.

And here I was running away from her because I couldn't think of a single thing to say to do that moment justice. I'd turned her pretty smile over in my head so many times, remembered the way she used to lock her fingers with mine whenever we watched a movie. She wasn't just most of my good memories—she was *all* of them. Every other part of my past was tainted with pain. But not her. She didn't know it then, but she kept me breathing all those nights when it felt like the end of the world was just around the corner.

Blades of stubborn wheatgrass whipped against the rough denim of my jeans as I lifted the bottle over my head, swallowing deep as the lovely liquid burned away the pain of seeing her face again. The sweet contours even prettier than I remembered, full lips that'd taunted me so many nights begging for a taste. Whiskey-laced irises haunting my dreams.

I cussed when my boots hit mud, the soft sound of the sucking like a playlist for how this entire night had gone. Water lapping a shoreline lifted my gaze to a small lake, dark shadows playing off moonlight. The thud of my back hitting the old wooden bench was deaf on my ears as Augusta Belle danced around my thoughts, twisting with a whiskey bottle, fogging my head until the only thing I could do was take another drink.

The first night I ever tasted what would soon become my constant companion, she was lifting a half-empty bottle to my lips, urging me to taste.

"It won't hurt," she promised, *"too much." Her eyes glinted in the darkness of her upstairs bedroom, her breath already heavy with the scent of rebellion.*

"Your mom would never let me in this house again if she found us both drunk," I warned, always the cautious one between us.

"She'd never let you see me again if she found you up here in my room." That defiant twinkle again. If I was sure of anything else, it was that this girl was born to be a rebel. "Scared?"

Hell yes, I'd been scared then, but not of the liquid in that bottle. Scared of the hellfire and brimstone that was her.

I groaned, the memory fading as fast as it'd come.

What in the fuck was Augusta Belle doing back in my life, walking up one day like a ghost? The very ghost that'd sheared my heart wide open and then found its way on to the radio for everyone to feel.

I groaned, throwing back the last of the amber whiskey and dropping the bottle at my feet.

Some fucking foresight that I hadn't brought a backup

bottle.

I'd also had the bitter taste of regret in my mouth about that single I'd signed off on with the music execs in Nashville.

I remembered the meeting only in chunks.

The bitter smell of the chain coffee shop. The green tie loosened at head-douchebag's collar.

I'd hated both of them from the minute I'd sat down.

But I was a stupid kid with a broken heart and an aimless shuffle in my feet.

"Over a million views on YouTube, you've really accomplished something." His eyes'd sliced up and down my haggard body. I hadn't had a shower in a few days, singing dive bars all night for tips and then drinking my earnings away till dawn.

It'd only been luck that Augusta Belle had created the YouTube channel, after I'd dragged my feet for months, and uploaded a few of my songs. There were some with her singing backup off-screen, the warmth of her encouragement surrounding me as I strummed and sang my heart out in my bedroom.

And then she'd vanished.

Left me in the dust. For what, I still wasn't sure. Coulda been dead in another river for all I knew.

Augusta Belle had been gone a week when I uploaded the last song.

The song that flayed my heart open.

The song I still couldn't sing onstage without something heavy clawing at my throat.

Never would have guessed her coming back could be any more painful than her leavin', but so it was.

The irony wasn't lost on me that the channel she'd made for me was the very thing that launched the name Fallon Gentry into headlines.

I was so fucking innocent, using my real name, but I don't think either one of us thought that humble little channel would get any attention.

But that was all in the past. I'd called my sister the day I crossed the Nashville city limits all those years ago, given her the password and insisted she shut down the account.

The videos still floated around. I had no control over them, but I did have some sort of control of my public persona. It didn't take long before the writing was on the wall for me. I didn't want a damn thing to do with anything in the public eye.

Making my music my business had been the gravest mistake of my life. Suddenly the business overshadowed all else, and I'd lost the very thing that'd brought me there in the first place.

Her.

It'd been a few years and a few thousand miles since then, and I was sure I'd seen the darkest corner of every country-rock bar south of the Mason-Dixon. Singing on a lonely stage, locals in every city all the same—tolerate the music, stay for the booze.

My life was simple.

Well, it had been.

Until Augusta Belle.

How this woman had the ability to throw me way the fuck off-kilter whenever I was in her orbit still amazed and annoyed me.

I pushed a rough hand over my face, multiple months' worth of unkempt beard making me laugh out loud.

Augusta Belle hadn't seen me with a beard, don't even think I'd been able to grow one back then, but here I was looking all lumberjacked.

The first time we'd met, I'd been scrawny, legs not bigger than twigs and biceps a fraction of the size I had now. I'd grown big, scary, a little wild-looking, all on account of keepin' the TMZ bitches off my back. Sellin' a picture wasn't much good when the subject was about unrecognizable and flippin' the bird.

They hadn't bothered me once since I'd left Nashville. Thank fuck.

That was the last thing I needed to deal with right now.

Augusta Belle was back, for better or worse. The woman I'd written a #1 hit about was in possession of the keys to my truck, and maybe still my heart.

I kicked back on the bench, damp wood cradling my

broken body as more memories of us washed over me like a tidal wave.

The first time I met her, she was fixin' to throw herself off a bridge. How could I have thought that life after meeting Augusta Belle Branson would be anything but extraordinary ever again?

THREE

Fallon—Twelve Years Before

"Mind if I ask what you're doing up here, lookin' all sad?" I stepped closer, knowing damn well the look of desperation in her eye.

Couldn't say I hadn't felt like that a few times myself.

"Admirin' the view." The sweet twang in her words made me smile. "Which I'd like to do in peace, if you don't mind."

I stifled a laugh with the back of my hand.

Her eyes averted back to the slow-movin' water below. "Wonder how many people have jumped into that river."

"None that have made it, I'd venture to guess." I moved forward, hopin' to get in arm's reach of her in case she took a mind to throw herself over the side. "My pa used to tell me a story when I was a kid 'bout someone gettin' thrown off this bridge. I always thought he just said it to scare us." I inched nearer. "Pretty far down, and then the impact alone. Not a good way to go if you ask me."

Call it instinct, but I felt something in this girl was sad beyond words.

On the outside, she was sweet, a cascade of blond hair and eyes that twinkled with mischief. But behind that mischief, I recognized a tired soul.

A girl who'd seen too much in her short years on this planet.

"Not if you know how to dive. I'd be fine. But—" she sent me a side eye "—if I tried, you'd probably try something heroic like savin' me."

I arched an eyebrow, trying to think a step ahead of her. "Hafta."

I was finally close enough to catch her by the arm if she tried to pull a fast one.

"Can I ask a question?" I leaned close, forcing her gaze on mine.

"As long as it's not *Why would a pretty girl like you want to kill herself?*" She took a few steps to gain some distance, eyes on the rushing current again.

"Well, pardon me if that's the only thing on my mind. So?"

"So? You can be more creative than that." She was moving closer to the center of the bridge now.

"Fine. Doesn't the finality of it scare you?"

"What?" Warm walnut eyes hovered on mine.

"Y'know, killin' yourself. It's so final. What if you just woke up on the wrong side of the bed this morning? Happens to me all the time. I don't think about killin' myself, though. If anything, I just stay in bed and play guitar all day, take a time-out."

"So…" She crossed her arms, tilting her head to one side, "You're questioning my decision-making?"

I nodded. "You're about the saddest lookin' girl I've ever seen, so absolutely."

She furrowed her forehead, locking her fists on the rusted railings of the old bridge. "Well, my mind's made up. I appreciate your efforts at—"

"Saving your life?" I interjected.

"Right. That." The tip of one flip-flop hung out on the lowest rung now. "But there's a lot you're not privy to, and I'd really appreciate it if you could just carry on with your day and leave me to mine." Both feet on the lowest rung now. Shit, she was really going to do it.

"I'm Fallon." I jumped across the space that separated us and thrust out my hand.

She arched one quizzical eyebrow before nodding. "Augusta Belle Branson, nice to meet you."

She smiled once, and in the next blink, she disappeared.

"Fuck," I grumbled under my breath. "Know your

name. Have to save you now."

I kicked off my heavy boots, knowin' they'd weigh me down, then gripped the railing and hurled myself over after her.

The trip to the muddy water below wasn't as far as I'd made it out to be, and I was in the slow-moving current within seconds. I bobbed out of the water, hands moving to feel for any human body under the murky depths around me.

"Augusta!" I called, swimming a few strokes to the cement pilings that held the bridge above the river. Shit, maybe she'd hit her head or broken a leg when she'd fallen against a boulder hidden by the current.

I pushed the water out of my face, squinting against the bright rays of summer sunshine that tried to blind me. Nothing about this day was going to end well, and I'd already woken up with a splitting headache after the hell Dad had put all of us through last night.

The memory of words like *useless* and *no-good* not exactly the thing I wanted to be thinkin' about in my last moments.

"Augusta Belle Branson, if I find you, and there's a breath left in your body—"

"Are you threatening the victim now?" That honeyed twang warmed my insides.

I spun in the water, seeing her crawl up the bank, cotton clinging to her skinny legs.

Jesus, soakin' wet and she couldn't have been more than an even hundred pounds. And she was younger than I'd thought. What kind of shit had driven her here?

I swam to the shoreline, grabbing one of the limestone edges and heaving myself onto the warm stone. "Mind if I ask what the fuck that was about?"

A wry grin curved her lips as she avoided my eyes.

"Good to scare yourself a little every day, I think."

My gaze locked on hers, that haunted, sad cloud still hovering just beyond the sarcasm. "Scared doesn't even begin to cover it."

I shielded my eyes from the unforgiving sun, guessing it wasn't even noon yet. "That's a lot of excitement so early on a Sunday morning. Mind if we take a breather while you tell me the real reason you threw yourself like a rag doll off the highest bridge in Chickasaw Ridge?"

She slumped into a sopping wet pile next to me. "Grew up swimmin' here, and really, it's not as high as it looks. If you throw yourself off the Whiskey River Bridge expectin' to meet God, you'd better have the right spot scoped out. You can see clear through to the bottom in most parts. I've jumped off all the bridges on the Whiskey River."

I had to suppress a groan. "Of course you have."

"What's that mean?" She pulled out a stick of gum, offered it to me, then popped it in her mouth when I refused.

"I hate to think of what's next if it takes jumpin' bridges to thrill you now at…how old are you?"

She stopped chewing the gum, expressive eyes leveled on mine. "Nunya."

"Are conversations with you always this… informative?"

She grinned, chewed the gum, and then twisted the end around her ring finger, stretching the goo and then snapping it back into her mouth. "Only with strangers."

"Interesting. Even strangers who save your life?"

"News flash, dude. Didn't need saving." She inched closer to the ledge, dipping one red-painted toe in the dark water.

"But I was willin' to. And let's not forget you told me your name before you launched over like a bat out of hell." I shrugged. "Thought that meant we were friends. Which, you see, obligated me to go in after you."

She ticked her head to the side, lips curving. "Fine." She slugged me in the bicep. "I'll give you that one."

I suppressed the urge to eye roll before she turned back to the murky water. "Hope we don't get a flesh-eating disease out of that muddy cesspool."

Augusta Belle's laughter carried on the wind, leaves rustling around us before the sun ducked behind a cloud, casting a chill. She shivered, running her palms up her tiny upper arms.

"We should go get changed. I can walk you home if

you want." I held out a hand.

She glanced at my outstretched palm, licks of dark ink peeking out from under my sleeve. Her eyes closed for a breath before they landed back on the water again, and she shook her head. "I'm good here. The sun will be back."

I dropped my hand, studying her profile, wondering again what brought a girl like her up here.

Maybe I was wrong, maybe she hadn't exactly been plannin' on killin' herself, so she said anyway. But that didn't shake the cloud of sadness that cast a shadow in those pretty eyes.

"Gonna make me stay here all day and babysit you from jumping back in that river?" I teased, dipping my toes in alongside her.

"Babysit?" She cast me a sideways glare. "Hardly. But you are welcome to hang out. It just so happens I think you're worthy of my company because, y'know, you tried to save me and all. Figure we were meant to be friends."

"That so?"

She nodded without glancing at me. "No one ever goes up on that bridge since the Tallahatchie was built. That's why I picked it." Her honey-brown irises lingered on mine. "While everyone was singin' in church, sending their praise above, I was supposed to be floatin' in that river. But I'm not. You know why? Because of you, Fallon Gentry. Of all the days, of all the moments, you showed up in my life."

She wrapped her tiny fingers around my wrist and tugged me a little closer to her.

I huffed, pretendin' she wasn't havin' the effect on me she did. "I don't care what your stupid ass does on your own time, but you're not dying on mine, Augusta Belle Branson."

FOUR

Fallon

A woodpecker hammering at the inside of my head finally had my eyes fluttering to life.

I pushed a hand over my face, taste of whiskey still on my breath as bolts of violent sunlight streaked my eyelids.

"Christ," I groaned, trying to twist away the pain in my lower back when I landed with a thunk on the wet ground below me.

The bench.

The bar.

The girl.

"Fuck me."

I pulled the empty bottle out from under my back, groaning as I slowly peeled myself off the muddy grass and stumbled to my feet.

The memories of last night were fighting at my consciousness, memories of the past haunting my brain as if I'd relived them all again last night.

I s'pose I had.

One by one.

The movie of our lives played out right there on that bench, ticket for one.

Morning was the worst time of day for me, too early to pour another drink, mind too goddamn foggy to keep the past at the door for long.

I walked slowly back across the field, following the swampy tracks I'd marched in on, the journey a helluva lot easier without a bottle in my hand.

The bar was probably only a mile down the road. I sure as hell knew I hadn't walked that far last night.

And what did I expect to find when I got there?

A goodbye letter tucked under the windshield wiper of my truck?

Maybe.

Gouges out of all four of my tires?

Possibly.

What I did find once I'd made the trek back was about the furthest possibility on my list.

Hadn't even occurred to me.

Augusta Belle Branson.

Perched on my stage.

My guitar in hand.

Singin' prettier than a songbird, half a dozen alcoholics hangin' on her every word.

I hated her even more than I had five minutes ago.

"What the fuck is this?" I gritted out, pausing at the dimly lit bar. "Why's she got my guitar?"

The bartender, who'd I'd been slippin' twenties the last few nights to keep the drinks coming while I sang, just shrugged and trained his eyes back on my girl.

My girl.

A low growl tore past my lips. "She's always fuckin' with my stuff. Gonna put an end to this. Make me a Bloody Mary for when I get back, wouldya?" I tapped the wooden bar once before stomping off through the tangle of round tables and right up onstage as Augusta Belle crooned the last lines of her song.

Everyone clapped, a few whistles and hollers of appreciation before I snatched the guitar, *my guitar*, from her hands and slung it over my back. "Whaddya think you're doin'?"

She tilted her head to one side, those warm brandy eyes swimming with curiosity, contempt, a mixture maybe, until she finally said, "You look like hell."

Damn, she looked even prettier in the morning. What I said instead was, "Good thing I give zero fucks what you think. Got my truck keys?"

I'd always been a real charmer.

She stood from the stool, pushing a hand into her pocket and fishing out the familiar set. "Sure you're not still drunk?"

"I'm 'bout to be." I swiped the keys from her palm and shoved them deep into my pocket, safe from her.

"You're drinking again?" She was quick on my heels as I headed back to the bar for my breakfast. Or lunch, as it were.

The pounding in my head had grown to DEFCON levels. "What's that?" I tossed over my shoulder. "A high-pitched wail with a Southern accent in my ear fillin' my head with shit?"

I paused at the bar. "Where's my Bloody Mary?"

"She told me to cut you off."

"What!" I spun on her, mouth twisted. "I hardly know her. If I don't get that Bloody Mary, I won't get my daily serving of vegetables. It's my salad, man."

"You're such a baby." Augusta Belle looped her arm in my elbow and pulled me off the bar, dragging me ass-backward out the front door and into the warm afternoon air.

"Hate your fucking hands on me," I said, a visceral reaction down deep finally bubbling out.

"Fallon—"

"Don't fucking *Fallon* me," I husked at her ear. Without thinking, my hands landed at her inner elbows, tightening slowly, pulling her up nice and close to my hard chest. "You lost the right to give a goddamn when you left."

Her dark eyes hung heavy on mine, soft contours of her neck flexing as she swallowed. Tears welled up in her beautiful, stubborn eyes before she started to speak. "Fuck you, Fallon Gentry."

I laughed off her curse, murmuring into the curve of her tender neck. "So sweet. So vulnerable, heartbeat racing like a brand-new bird."

I grazed my lips along the edge of her ear, delighting when aroused shivers followed in my wake. "I could slide in deep, fuck you raw until you forget where I end and you begin, couldn't I, Augusta Belle? Anything for a piece of the country boy turned superstar, is that it? Next, you're gonna tell me you were thinkin' we could start a band, some John and Yoko bullshit." I tightened my grip at her arms. "At one point, I thought you were *dead*"—the last word a sneer—"and when I found out you weren't, I wished it."

I released her arms, pushing away from her body and turning on my boot heel, gravel crunching as I strode to my truck.

"Fallon!" she called, the word nearly lost on the wind.

I paused at my truck, hand hovering on the door before I took an extra second and turned to look at her, commit her to memory one last time.

She stood in the parking lot, just as I'd left her, but this

38

time, her arms were wrapped around her waist and tears tracked down her cheeks.

"Christ." I suppressed the roll of my eyes before I shoved both hands into my pockets and went back to her. "Jesus, Augusta, don't fucking cry."

Her usually pretty pink lips twisted into something angry, ruthless. "If you think I tracked you all the way out here to this hellhole just to get in bed with you, then you have changed."

"Changed?" I roared, fists balling with anger in my pockets. "I've changed? You disappear for ten years, and you're telling me *I've* changed? I used to think if you waltzed back into my life, I'd take you back without question. But now that you're here, Augusta, I've got a fuck of a lot of questions. So many fucking questions I've been drownin' them in whiskey tryin' to chase them out of my head. I let that pain marinate real good. Only thing I could find to help me heal."

"Heal?" She breathed. "This is you healed?" Her brows knitted together. "I'd hate to see the before."

My glare refused to unchain her, head shaking. "Where the fuck did you *go*, Augusta?"

FIVE

Augusta—Twelve Years Before

"Stuck! I feel stuck, you bastard! You ruined all the best parts of me, you and that freeloading *daughtah*. If Mama would've left me *everythin'* like she promised, bet your ass I wouldn't be here right now…" The carefully manufactured sadness lacing my mother's voice never ceased to drive me to the brink of insanity.

Did she think we felt bad for her?

She'd grown up wealthy, of the *genteel* class, as she always said. But she'd squandered her inheritance on priceless art and Vicodin, as far as I could tell. And now she spent her days blaming us. The low baritone of my father's tired, vodka-slurred words echoed up the stairs, losing their stamina as I descended out of my upstairs window. My fingertips clutched at the roof's edge, dirty

Converse covering my bare feet as I launched off the roof and landed on the soft earth.

Moonlight lit the fields of bluegrass in silver, highlighting the stately white pillars that anchored the wide wraparound porch of the home I'd grown up in. I snuck through the line of hemlocks that flanked either side of our driveway, picking my way along the shadows until I was confident I was out of sight, and earshot, of the house at 101 River Ridge Drive.

I skipped past the trail that led through the woods and out onto the ridge overlooking the river, and I headed for Fallon's house. I'd done this walk at midnight so many times, I could find my way along the twists and turns of the old country road with my eyes closed.

I was surprised by the liking I'd taken to Fallon Gentry.

Something about the way he'd watched over me when he thought I was about to jump off the bridge. I'd known then we'd be friends.

I don't know if it was fate that found Fallon up there on that bridge at the same time as me, but from the moment we met, we seemed to be savin' each other.

Dark clouds shadowed the moon as I sped up my steps, more anxious than ever to get to Fallon and not be so…*alone.*

While it might have been true that I lived at 101 River Ridge Drive with both of my parents, most days I'd rather I lived alone over listening to them spew the hatred they did. Their example of marriage had me ruling it out for the rest of eternity. Sneaking out to Fallon's house since he'd sorta saved my life on that bridge had become my saving grace.

"Hundred and two days," I said a few minutes later when he opened the window.

"What?" A wild lick of hair fell in front of one eyebrow. My fingers itched to push it away. I resisted.

"That's how long we've known each other. Hundred and two days. I counted."

He looked behind him once before climbing out of his bedroom window. "How long'd that take ya?"

"Shut up." I launched my fist into his bicep, and he laughed.

I loved his laugh. Like, really loved it.

I swear, sometimes it woke me up out of my fantasies in the middle of the night.

And if I was lucky, it was reality.

More than once, I'd fallen asleep in Fallon's arms, too tired to go home. The comfort of his warm body and the cool quilt pulling me under. I slept the most peacefully in Fallon's arms, there was no doubt about it. And not just because Mom and Dad weren't in my ear hollering all night, but because being with him was as easy as being me.

There'd been a few close calls, but it hadn't taken me

long to realize that Mom didn't even check on me before school in the morning, and Dad was already out the door long before I woke up. I was free from ten o'clock till six in the morning, easily.

"So what's going down at *Chez la Branson* tonight?" The gravelly edge in his voice twisted my insides upside down. Fallon definitely had a rebel, bad-boy thing about him, a few too many tattoos for the likes of Chickasaw Ridge, but I think they fit him perfectly, plus he'd told me each of the stories behind them. They were art, an extension of him.

I huffed, looping my arm in his elbow and trailing him down the mossy path to the edge of the field. "I think she knows about Iris."

"The mistress?" Fallon's warm hand wrapped around mine, filling all the lonely holes in my heart almost instantly. "Why?"

"Mom saw some emails." I was thankful when Fallon dropped under the first oak tree we came to that bordered the field, throwing his jacket on the grass so we could lie on it.

He nestled me back into his chest, adjusting me easily, before his nose tucked into my hair and he sucked in a soft breath. "They been fighting?"

"Yeah," I breathed, stubborn tears pricking my eyelids. "More than usual."

"S'okay, Ms. Branson, that just means more time for

us."

Us.

I loved when he said that word, rolling it off his tongue and pooling in my insides like warm butter.

"I just wish they didn't make my ears bleed."

"I've heard them go at it. Think I'd set up a tent and camp out in the yard if I had to listen to that all the time." He pulled me a little tighter, that still-too-long lock of dark hair whispering at his eyebrow, begging for me to tuck it where it belonged.

"You gonna get a haircut anytime soon?"

One eyebrow shot up, and a cocky grin danced across his face. "Not as long as you keep askin' me about it. Better to stand out for something than nothin' at all."

I pursed my lips, digging deeper into his hard chest.

"And as for the other stuff, you'll get through. You're the toughest girl I know, Augusta Belle."

"Toughest?" I tried to keep any ounce of desperate hope out of my voice. "You once said I was the saddest girl you've ever met. That still true?"

"Truer now than it ever was." Fallon held a fingertip to my hairline at my temple, a sad grin settling on his lips. "I'd save you if I could."

"You already have," I whispered, tears pricking at the backs of my eyelids as I sucked in a breath of the cool night air, praying for at least the thousandth time that something would happen to make my parents see that all the fighting wasn't just destroying the other, it was destroying me too.

And then Fallon Gentry had shown up.

Sometimes I thought God sent him to be the answer to my prayers.

I didn't even know if I believed in God, but maybe I should start if it meant more good things like Fallon would start popping up in my life.

"Saving you is the pleasure of my life, Augusta Belle."

A stubborn trail of salty hope fell down my cheek as I focused on the soft rising and falling of Fallon's chest.

"Love you, Fallon Gentry. One of these days you're gonna be a star and leave this town, and I'll still be sitting here, under this tree, wondering where my white knight went."

"Enough daydreaming, you've got school in the morning. What kinda boyfriend would I be if I didn't get you to school on time?"

"Boyfriend?" I swallowed the sudden ball of nerves in my throat. "Really?"

"Well…" His fingers stroked the underside of my wrist and sent goose bumps skittering in every direction. "Figure we've been actin' like it…"

"Does that mean I have to wash your laundry or anything?" He shook his head, awkward grin slipping into the familiar crooked one I was used to. "You make me want to skip school."

"You can't. If you're not there, you can't graduate, which means you can't move out of that house, which would make you doomed to hell forever."

I huffed, hating how right he always was. "What kinda girl would I be anyway if I accepted an offer from the first guy who came along, one who didn't even know my birthday?" I countered.

"Fine." His fingers threaded through mine, cementing our physical connection. "Does this mean you're finally going to tell me how old you are?"

I pressed my teeth into my bottom lip, eyes glinting as our gazes held. "July nineteenth."

His face turned into a scowl. "You know, in a few keystrokes I could find out everything you never wanted me to know."

"But you won't." My breaths began to match his, eyelids growing heavier with each passing moment.

"How can you be so sure?"

"Because," I yawned. "You like me too much to piss me off. And where's the fun in me telling you everything anyway?"

"I swear, Augusta Belle…"

SIX

Fallon

"I swear, Augusta Belle, if you don't make me madder than a goddamn hatter." I stomped across the parking lot, hand pushing through my hair and dead set on the last swallows of a nearly dry bottle of Jack that I knew was kicking around the back of my truck.

"Agh! That's not even what that means!" she screamed. "You mean—"

I spun, retracing my bootsteps and catching her chin between my fingers before she could finish her sentence. "You lost the right to tell me what I mean ten years ago."

She narrowed her eyes, jaw hardening as she pulled herself out of my reach. "You want to know what happened to me back in Chickasaw Ridge, Fallon?" Her normally singsong voice was threaded with fire. "You think you're ready for that?"

"You think you're ready for what the fuck happened to me? You're still the selfish little girl I used to know if you think you're the only one who was affected by you leaving."

"I didn't leave." Her voice was suddenly quiet, but the ferocity in her eyes still flaring bright.

She was even more gorgeous when she was angry. Still didn't know what the fuck I had done to deserve this kind of torture.

I thought running from her memory had been hell, but it was here. Five-foot-two and mad as a motherfucker, rooted in front of me now.

"I didn't leave, Fallon. You should know that." Her voice was nearly a whisper.

"How the hell would I know anything?" I tossed my arms in air, mind out of control as the possibilities warred within me. "Christ, I thought you were dead, and can ya blame me? Wouldn't have been the first time." She narrowed her eyes, and I knew my arrows had hit their mark.

"Done yet?" The chill in her voice rattled my bones.

Bitterness rose in my throat, that whiskey bottle calling my name louder than ever. "Just gettin' started, sweetheart."

I turned back to my truck, pulling the door open when a flash of black sped past my head, followed by a pair of red Converse stepping up onto the running board.

Augusta Belle and her backpack were perched in the front seat.

I ducked out of the back, muscles tremoring with need for the numb escape they were used to, knocking my head against the frame as I went. "Fuck!"

"You shouldn't allow yourself to get so stressed. Not good for your health, and the way you're already taxing that liver…"

"Jesus, what did I do to deserve this?" The slow pounding in my head grew to a deafening decibel. "You're not coming with me, Branson. No fucking way."

"Sure am." The confident grin gracing her face boiled my insides.

"No—" I yanked her backpack out of the car and held it in the air "—you're not." I dropped the backpack in the dust at my feet, then climbed into the truck. "Now, get out."

"Not going anywhere." She crossed her arms, settling in.

"Oh, for fuck's sake." I kicked the door open, throwing myself out, boots first. "Why the hell not?"

"Aw." Her eyes whipped up and down my form, drawn tighter than a crossbow. "You look like a spoiled schoolboy with your hands on your hips like that." She tilted her head, blond waves falling over one shoulder. "Or my mother."

I growled, dropping my hands to my sides, stupidly self-conscious for the first time…well…since the last time I saw Augusta Belle.

I trekked around the front of my truck, throwing the passenger door open and climbing up into the cab, lips hovering just out of reach of her succulent, pert, stubborn-as-hell little mouth. "Please leave, Augusta." My palm pushed up the curve of her thigh, soft, worn denim rubbing against my fingertips and grating on every last nerve. "Don't make me do something we'll both end up regretting."

The delicate little concave indentation of her throat flexed as she swallowed before her head began a slow shake. "I didn't come this far to have you drive off into the sunset, booze in hand, without even talkin' to me."

"And how far did you come, exactly?" I pressed an inch higher, hovering just out of reach of the top of her thigh, eyes burning up the space between us.

"Not far." She swallowed again. "You think I'd let you come anywhere near the state of Tennessee and not hunt you down?"

The fog cleared for a minute, whiskey haze burning off for the first time in days. "I don't even know what town I'm in."

A small huff pushed past her lips. "Figures. Cherry Valley? Tennessee?" She waited for me to say something. But instead, I hovered silently, unpacking the years it'd been since I'd crossed the Tennessee state line.

Heady peaches and honey filled my memories as the feeling of home settled over me. I guess in the back of my mind somewhere I knew I was in Tennessee, but these hills and hollers all looked the same after a lot of late nights playing music. The notion that she was back hadn't even occurred to me. The Bransons never had family outside of Chickasaw Ridge that I'd heard about, so when she'd disappeared, she'd vanished and left me without a trail to follow. "Where you living?"

Her little hand grazed my bicep. Made me angry how this woman's touch still had that same old thrilling effect on me. "I'm back home. For now. Workin' on puttin' the house up for sale."

"Oh." I moved away, pushing a hand through my hair and letting the knowledge that her parents had probably passed settle in.

"I'm desperate for a shower, though. Your next stop is in Memphis according to your website, so that should only take us a few hours if we get on the road."

"Wait, I have a website?" I plopped down on the seat beside her. She scooched, making room for my big body. Still, our bodies touched, elbows rubbing, thighs kissing. I settled one arm across the seat behind her, reminding me just how easy it was, being with her. Not a thing changed. Except everything. Some errant lightning stroke of pain struck my heart thinkin' about all we'd been through, wonderin' if there was even a possibility of starting over for us.

I didn't think so.

Augusta Belle Branson had torn my heart from my chest. No way was I letting that thief back inside.

"Tons of websites. The Fallon fangirls are still loud and proud. But I also talked to your sister," Augusta stated. "Said she hasn't talked to you in almost a year, beyond a text once in a while. I'm afraid to ask, but is this what you've been doing? Playin' music at night and drinkin' and drivin' all day? Because if that's the case, you need me even more than I thought."

"No." Realization that it was exactly what I'd been doing went down like a jagged pill. "Not *all* day. And I don't need your shit. I'm doing fine." The words were hollow even as I said them.

I jumped out of the truck, heading around the front and tossing her backpack into the cab before climbing behind the wheel and turning over the engine. "I'll take you to Memphis, but that's it. After that, you and me, us —" I pointed back and forth between us "—ends."

Her face fell a fraction, but she recovered quickly. Someone else may not have caught it, but even after all these years, it felt like I knew her better than the back of my hand.

Augusta Belle Branson was embedded like barbed wire around my soul.

SEVEN

Fallon

"I wanna break away…be myself sometime…but all I see is pouring rain…all I get is more of your pain…" My fingers tapped out an absent rhythm against the steering wheel, my mind matching a melody to the somber words that'd been playin' in my head the last few days. *"You only get a little while to shine before you fade away…but out here on the highway, your ghost is more than I can take…"*

"That's beautiful." Augusta breathed, reminding me she was there.

Hell.

I'd done a damn good job ignoring her the first thirty minutes on the road. So well she'd stopped asking me about myself and minded her own damn business.

I flipped on the radio, cycling through a few country

stations before I settled on a Johnny Cash song.

"You gonna talk to me at all this trip?"

I shook my head, lips tight, eyes trained on the pavement.

She groaned, adjusting in her seat before she unbuckled her seat belt, turning in the cab and reaching for her backpack. I heard the zipper a moment later before she yanked the long-sleeved shirt off her torso and balled it up, throwing it behind her. She appeared front and center on my bench seat a second later, toothbrush and toothpaste in hand. "Can we stop at a rest area? I have to brush my teeth. I didn't have cash to stay at a hotel last night, which means no sink to brush my teeth this morning. Y'know that furry feeling your teeth get? Yeah, that's what I'm dealing with right now."

"Hang on, where did you sleep last night?" I finally broke my silence. Begrudgingly.

"I could ask you the same thing." She buckled herself into the seat next to me, elbows rubbing, thighs kissing again. Just like when we were young.

I hated that I kept thinking that.

Augusta Belle and I were two totally different people. Always had been. Different sides of the tracks. Whatever we were to each other for that brief moment in time was what we'd needed. But not anymore. Not ever again.

"Slept out under the stars. I do it now and again. Good for the constitution, Pa used to say."

"Sure." I caught the roll of her eyes.

"And you slept where?" I urged.

"Your truck."

I nearly veered into opposing traffic. "What?"

"Where else was I supposed to go? And you were generous enough to leave me with your keys, so—"

"I didn't leave you my keys. You stole them!"

She shrugged, punching at the radio tuner once and letting it settle on a Reba song. "This is my favorite."

"Always has been," I said instantly, remembering the first time I heard her sing along to the words, sitting beside me just like this as we drove up the ridge, destination set on a new bridge this time.

Everything about Augusta Belle drew me in, a tantalizing beauty meant to entice me into signing over my fucking soul.

She may have lanced me with her poison-tipped blade once, but not again. Not ever again.

EIGHT

Fallon—Eleven Years Before

She cuddled up against me, the little polka-dot triangles of her bathing suit top fuller than they had been last summer. The summer I'd found her swan-diving into the Whiskey River like some fearless mermaid, hell-bent on rebellion and stealin' my soul on the way. From the second I'd laid eyes on her, something had fascinated me. And now that'd we'd spent nearly every day together for almost the last year, I could say it was her fearless bravery that drove me to her. Watching her like a rare bird when every other person in this town was trying to be the same.

"Which bridge this time?" I turned my truck toward the river.

She cocked her head to the side, sun glinting in a halo

around the crown as she tucked her leg under herself and grinned. "Pine Bluff."

"But that one's the highest," I protested weakly, knowing she'd already made up her mind.

"Listen, Fallon Gentry, no use riding shotgun your whole life. Sometimes you just have to jump." Her eyes twinkled before she launched herself into my lap and pressed her honey-sweet lips to mine in a kiss.

I pushed a hand in her hair, the soft rocking of her hips against mine driving my control to the very edge of my sanity. "We're almost there."

"Don't stop kissing me," she begged, something new, exciting, heavy with the scent of adrenaline coursing through her bloodstream. In all the nights we'd spent together, slept together, we'd never done more than just kiss. Not because I didn't want to; I wanted to be with her in every way a guy wants to be with his girlfriend. But I wasn't willing to take anything from her she wasn't a thousand percent ready to give.

And no matter how many times she tried to convince me she was ready, she wasn't.

"I can't see, crazy girl." I caught glimpses of the dirt road, tree-lined and all but vacant at the height of heat on a June afternoon.

"Just keep going straight. I can see the reflection in the back window. I'll let you know when to turn."

My growl of frustration deepened when she rocked

her hips harder against my aching body, strung tight and praying for every last thread of control.

"Augusta Belle…" I pleaded, unable to keep my eyes from slamming closed when the seam of her damp denim cutoffs made contact with my aching erection.

"Do you trust me?" She nipped at my earlobe, dainty fingertips crawling up my neck as she pushed against me, digging the core of her hot little body against every square inch of mine.

"Always." The word came out desperate.

"I'm ready, Fallon," she whispered. "I'm ready for us."

I swallowed, brain hopping violently to a dozen various conclusions as one of my hands gripped the wheel, the other tightening on her round ass cheek through her shorts. My heart thundered like a thousand wild horses as I thought about sliding between her legs for the first time, touching her warm body, making love to every square inch of the woman who kept me awake at night.

"Turn!" she shrieked, pulling herself off my lap just before an old dump truck laid on its horn, careening sideways to avoid my little truck and lodging my heart fully into my throat.

"Fuck." I pulled to the side of the road, hands white-knuckling the wheel.

"See? You can trust me," she chirped, pushing her door open and climbing out into the haze of dust left in the truck's wake.

"Trust you? I almost killed us a second ago." I switched off the engine of my truck and crawled out on shaky legs, coming around the side of the cab to find Pine Bluff Bridge stretching off into the distance.

"Woulda been a good way to go though, right?"

"Augusta Belle, no. No, it wouldn't be a good way to go. Why do you always talk about death as if it doesn't matter?"

One shoulder lifted haphazardly. "Want me to drive the rest of the way? I can see your nerves are a little rattled…"

I glared at her, at a legitimate loss for words.

"Or…I could just jump here? It's not that high up, although I haven't really scoped the boulder situation."

"What if I don't want you to jump at all? Can't we just sit here and take in the view? Maybe give me a second to recover from my first near-death experience."

"First?" She cast me a charming grin. "That's your second. First was when you jumped off the Whiskey River Bridge to sorta, kinda, but not really save my life, right?"

I shook my head, pulling down the tailgate of my truck and throwing an old blanket I kept in back out over the rusted metal bed. "Come."

Her eyes flared once before shifting across the little nest I'd made and back to me. "Okay."

She crossed the dirt parking lot, and I threaded her fingers with mine when she was close enough. I lifted her into the back, making sure she was comfortable before following her in.

"Is that all it took to get you into bed? A near-death experience?" She pressed her bikini-clad body up against mine, trying to wiggle ever closer.

"Calm those hormones, sunshine. No one's gettin' in anyone's bed." I adjusted her under my arm.

The soft little pout that pulled down her lips made me want to kiss her.

The age gap between us never seemed greater than when she was pouting for something I wouldn't give her.

Only lately, what she'd been wanting and I'd been withholding was sex.

"Told you I'm not taking your virginity until the time is right."

"Well, when in the hell is that gonna be? I might as well start calling you Saint Fallon." She pushed up on her forearms, legs swinging off the tailgate as she attempted to ignore me.

I laughed, sliding to the edge with her and grazing her shoulder. "Nothing saintly about me, I just want what's right for you. Also, don't want to give your mama and daddy an excuse to put me in jail. And if they found out how old I really was…"

"They won't. Dad just spends his time watching old

COPS episodes and reliving the glory days. And Mom hasn't left the house since before we met."

"Doesn't change the law, Augusta Belle. And while you may be stubborn enough to lie about your age—"

"It's not lying." She screwed up her face at me.

"Lying by omission is lying." I corrected her.

"Plus, I just had a birthday," she defended.

"I know, and you made me celebrate with you without once telling me how old you were turning."

She shrugged again, amber gaze turning back to the river that flowed down below us. "I operate on a need-to-know basis, and I'm still not convinced that's something you need to know."

I didn't bother rolling my eyes; I was used to her wordplay by this point.

"Sure, telling your twenty-two-year-old boyfriend is of no consequence at all."

She caught sight of me over her shoulder, flirty twinkle pulling me into her orbit a little further. "I'll tell you if you have sex with me."

I barked out a laugh. "The fact that you're willing to negotiate your virginity proves my point about waiting."

One delicate eyebrow arched up before she jumped off the tailgate, kicking off her flip-flops. She spun, nailing me with a radiant smile before looping her thumbs into her waistband and pushing the cutoffs down her thighs.

They landed in the dust at her feet a second later, and she kicked them off, then pushed her hands through her thick hair and wound it into a high bun. "Guess I'm going cliff-divin', then."

I pushed off the tailgate, closing the distance between us and pulling her into my arms, against my hard, imposing body. "How many times you gonna defy death before you realize what you're lookin' for is right here, Augusta Belle?"

She didn't answer, just let me keep her in my embrace for long minutes.

"Stop running and let me hold you."

NINE

Fallon

My mind careened violently out of the memory when a semitruck nearly drove straight up my tailpipe, and the driver pulled on his air horn.

"Your driving hasn't improved much, I see," Augusta Belle chimed in.

I grunted, casting her a glare before cranking up the volume on the radio, not giving a fuck what crappy, pop-infused country song was playing. Every mile closer we got to Memphis, the nearer I was to convincing myself a bottle in hand would make this drive a little easier. And then I got to thinkin' turning the fuck around and droppin' blondie off in Chickasaw might be my best idea yet.

"So..." She twisted the knob into the off position.

"There's something I need to tell you before we get to Memphis."

I narrowed my gaze. "Got a lot of things you need to tell me, far as I can tell."

"Yeah." I could see her fiddling with her fingers out of the corner of my eye.

"Spit it out."

"Right. Well, the reason I came to find you— —"

And here it was. The reason.

The big fucking reason it'd taken her ten years to track me down.

I didn't think I was prepared for it.

Didn't think I could stand the wait a second longer.

"See, when Daddy died this summer, I knew I couldn't stay in the house. It needs so much upkeep——"

"Fucking knew it." I cut her off.

"Knew what?" She paused, waiting for me to finish.

"Money. You need fucking money."

Her eyes flared before she licked her lips, bit down hard on the inside of her cheek, and then cocked her arm back and punched me solidly in the bicep.

"Ow. What the fuck?" I rubbed at the still stinging muscle.

"I don't need money, you asshole. And the way you just said that makes me want to jump out of this godforsaken truck right now and hitch a ride back to Chickasaw Ridge with a long-haul truck driver!"

I grunted, realizing none too late that I'd missed my mark and spoken too soon.

Her words held a serrated edge this time. "Daddy left *you* money. I don't know why—best I can recall, he never even liked you—but I think he knew… Well, he knew what you meant to me. I just came to track you down and tell you your share's waitin' in a safety deposit box in the Choctaw County Bank."

"I don't want it." The words came out bitterer than I'd meant them. "Use it to fix up the house."

"No." She shook her head, voice softening for the first time all day. "I can't spend a minute longer there than I have to, I have to get rid of it, and you have to help me. I hate it. Too many bad memories. Every time I try to remember the good times, you're always in them."

My heart stuttered to a slower beat, her words sinking in and melting away the barbed wire fences I'd built.

The cab hung heavy with silence for long minutes before I finally answered. "Why d'you need me to sell the house, Augusta?"

"Because." She barely breathed. "Daddy left that to you too."

TEN

Augusta—Eleven Years Ago

"Go be with your whore, then! Me'n Augusta'z bettah here anyway." My mother's Southern accent thickened in time with her intoxication. She was a few drinks in and freshly topped on her meds as far as the slurrin' indicated.

I pushed a finger through the neon pink concoction that coated the grocery store cupcake my mother had sent me upstairs with.

I sighed, licking the saccharine frosting off my finger.

"Christ, if I had to listen to this shit day in and out, I'd throw myself off the nearest bridge too."

"Shut up." I giggled just as Fallon snagged my wrist and pushed my finger into his mouth. His tongue rolled around the pad, and shivers raced down my spine, swirling in the bottom of my stomach.

I swallowed down the now familiar feeling of physical frustration I'd been dealing with whenever I was around Fallon Gentry. I'd always been attracted to him, the way his eyes followed me across a room, always readin' me like an open book.

But now he'd taken to working out.

His already broad chest was filling out, the hard slab of muscle bookended by biceps rock-hard enough to make my mouth water. And instead of the usual clean-shaven look I was used to, he now sported a regular five-o'clock stubble that made my fingers ache to touch.

"I don't remember a day in my life they haven't been fighting." I tossed the cupcake into the garbage can, smears of pink frosting running down the sides like unicorn tears. "Happy birthday to me."

Fallon scooped me in his heavy grip, snuggling me against him and into the mountain of white down pillows that swallowed my bed.

It was ironic. All the money spent on the fancy bed and linens to make me comfortable while I slept, and yet the only time my mind seemed to still was in his arms. It didn't matter where. Long as we were connected, I knew I was safe.

"'Nother trip around the sun, hmm?" Fallon's fingers threaded through mine as he turned over my wrist, dotting sweet kisses across the delicate veins and making butterflies batter all four of my heart's chambers.

"According to the birth certificate." Birthdays were never a pleasant event for me. I always felt too old for them, like the entire celebration of my birth was an occasion meant only to document their existence in future photo albums.

The fact that Dad had poured his first glass of vodka by six, as usual, and Mom was napping on the couch promptly fifteen minutes after eating half a slice of takeout pizza were only proof of my theory.

"So…" Fallon tipped my chin to catch my gaze. "Does that mean you get seventeen birthday kisses?"

My cheeks flamed, the idea of a make-out session more than my fragile heart could take. "How'd you know?"

He pressed his lips to mine, kissing me once before pulling away and smiling. "One." He stole another kiss at the opposite corner of my mouth. "It was a good guess. And two."

My heart spun in cartwheels, the idea that it'd been nearly a year and a half since Fallon had first found me up on that bridge a wild one. He'd saved me from myself —and the crazy parents 'who'd brought me into this world—plenty of times. All the nights stretched out under the stars, pointing out constellations and holding hands as the summer wind swept up our future hopes and dreams, carryin' 'em like music into the universe.

"Thank you," I finally breathed, choking up at the thought of my life without him.

His grin turned sideways, palms resting sweetly on either side of my face as his thumbs wiped away the quiet tears. "No thanks necessary." His lips caught more of my tears. "Loving you has been the pleasure of my life, Augusta Belle Branson."

I sobbed once, his too-kind words nearly breaking me apart.

"And I wouldn't be any kinda boyfriend at all if I didn't have somethin' to celebrate the day of your birth." He fished in his pocket before pulling out a slim envelope. "Isn't much, but every time I see it, I think of you. Figure that means it's meant for you." He opened the envelope, pulling out an antique gold chain connected to a tiny cameo with a mermaid perched right in the center. "Was my grandma's. My dad's got a pile of her stuff in the back bedroom. She loved to swim. Even now I remember going to her house as a kid and seeing all these swimming trophies and mermaids everywhere." He smiled, recalling memories of someone I knew meant so much. "My uncles used to shit on her for keeping all that stuff out everywhere, and she'd just wave them off and say she had to remember the good things in life before things like babies and bills came along. Mama said she meant it, though. Said she used to swim like she was part of the water."

He smiled, savoring some lost memory. "I never teased her. I thought it was cool, seeing her relive her dreams for just an instant each time she passed those shelves." His voice lowered another octave. "She's the only person who ever made me feel safe, protected, loved." Emotions churned in his moody, dark irises. "So every time I see a mermaid, it makes me smile."

"Come across mermaids often, huh?" I traced the delicate details of the pendant with my fingertips as it danced in the air between us.

"I do lately," he breathed, placing a kiss under my earlobe before hooking the chain around my neck. "You're my mermaid."

His fingers worked the clasp at the back of my neck, the soft drag of his fingers sending a riot of feelings tornadoing through my body.

"Thank you." I pressed the tiny trinket below my throat, the cool metal a constant reminder of his touch. His love.

"Someday you're gonna be a star, y'know." He kissed along my temples, down my cheekbones. "Gonna leave this town and go off to some fancy Ivy League university and forget the name Fallon Gentry. But I won't forget you." He placed kisses over both of my eyelids. "Fifteen, sixteen."

I smiled softly, regretting there was only one kiss left. "I'm not going anywhere, Fallon. I'm stuck here for as long as you are."

A sad smile danced in his eyes. "I won't let you."

I swallowed the growing lump in my throat, anxiety curling around my insides for the first time at the thought of leaving him. "Then you'll come with me."

He shook his head. "I'll make do, singing for tips while you get a full ride somewhere warm."

A ridiculous giggle pulled from my throat. "A full ride for what?"

"For swimming." He paused on my eyes, revealing he knew more than I thought he did.

I narrowed my eyes. "What makes you say that?"

He shrugged, breaking his warm gaze away from mine and giving my heart the tiniest of chills. "Saw the sports section of the *Morning Star*, Augusta Belle. You've broken all the state records. You're a star."

The lump in my throat had turned to molten lead, landing in the pit of my stomach and stealing the air from my lungs in the span of a single moment.

"It's just a hobby." I supposed he was going to find out my age at some point, find out I wasn't even a senior in high school. I'd refused to tell him my age when we met because I was only fifteen then, and he was older, much older. At least nineteen, if I would have guessed. Fortunately, at least back then, on the off chance my parents had caught me hanging out with Fallon, he looked younger. The clean-shaven face had helped, but lately…

Well, lately he was just a stone-cold fox.

"State-record holders aren't just practicing a hobby. Why didn't you tell me?" His eyes were trained on my lips, the pad of his thumbs stroking the ridge of my cheekbone.

"Because it's not a big deal."

"Everything about you is a big deal to me."

I chomped down on my bottom lip, wishing like hell he'd just touch me already. Push his hands between my thighs and make me his in all the ways. "What's on your mind, Augusta Belle?"

He trailed his nose along my hairline as he invaded every breath of my personal space and had me craving more.

"That you owe me one more birthday kiss."

His grin tipped up, fingers weaving into the mess of my hair at my neck before he pulled me closer, caging me against his heavenly body. "So I do."

Our lips connected, tongues pushing past all boundaries before he was hauling me onto him, my knees straddling his waist and our chests melding as he kissed me senseless and gave me the very best birthday of my life.

"I love you, Fallon."

"Love you more, Augusta Belle, even if you do drive me crazy most days." He tucked me into the crook of his shoulder, and I sucked in a heady breath of his scent.

"Thanks for being my friend."

He hushed me, fingertips trailing through the waves of my hair. "As I recall, you forced me up on that bridge that day."

I grinned, always grateful when he eased the heartache inside me with his characteristic levity. "So I did."

"That was the best day of my life."

"The day you almost sorta saved me?"

"The day I found the girl of my dreams." He hugged me closer, urging my eyes closed as I burrowed into the cotton of his t-shirt. "Happy birthday, Augusta Belle."

ELEVEN

Fallon

"Why would he leave the house to me?" I cleared my throat, trying to channel my insane sense of exasperation.

She shrugged, dipping a homemade French fry into her vanilla milk shake. "Dunno."

"Well, that just doesn't make any sense whatsoever, Augusta Belle. So you're gonna have to do a little more explainin' than that." I yanked the milk shake out of her hands and sucked on it myself.

She arched an eyebrow in challenge before swiping another fry through the creamy concoction and dotting some of it on my nose. "He changed a lot the last few years. Started opening up to me after Mom passed. She was diagnosed the same month I was supposed to

78

graduate college."

"You went to college?" I paused, lingering on all the things she might have made of herself. Law? Engineering?

"I'm a year's rotation short of being a physician's assistant." Her eyes flicked away, avoiding mine. "I moved home when Mama was diagnosed. Daddy couldn't take care of himself, much less her, and she faded quickly. I couldn't leave it all for him."

I set down the milk shake, the urge to pull her into my arms and comfort that sad look off her face strong. "Sorry 'bout that. Guess I still don't understand why he left me anything, though."

"He opened up about a lot of things. I was gone for so long, and by the time I came back, I think he thought of me as a different person. Told me one night he wished he could have done more to help you. I didn't know what he meant. Most of the time, he was too drunk to remember the next morning when I asked, so I took it with a grain of salt. Until I sat down with the lawyer. Until she said your name was in Daddy's will." She trained her gaze on me again, eyes heavy with unspoken questions.

"Your dad never talked to me. Didn't know my pa either, as far as I know." I shrugged, the memories of my past like more jagged pills gouging my throat on their way down. I swallowed the now familiar ache in my throat remindin' me it was 'round about that time when I'd be nursing my first glass. "Well, doesn't matter anyway. I don't want the money."

"I figured you'd say that." She scooted a little closer, knee brushing mine and making my heart leap erratically behind the wall of my chest. I winced, feeling the actual physical pain of having her so close and not being able to reach out and touch what was mine.

What had always been mine.

I swallowed the painful throb. "Why've you got that look like there's something else?"

"Because there's something else."

I winced again, not bothering to hide it this time. "Isn't there always with you?" I sighed, pretty sure I wasn't prepared for whatever was about to come next. "Go on."

"I came across this name in some papers in the attic." She rifled through her bag and thrust out a note, a stranger's name scrawled in fading blue ink. "I think I should meet her."

"Um." I paused, eyes wavering from the note back to her hopeful face. "That's probably just some chick your dad banged before he met your mom." I plucked the note from her hand and turned it over, looking for I wasn't sure what, and not finding it. "What does that have to do with me anyway?"

She frowned, pulling another stack of papers from her

backpack. "I found it with this."

My eyes blurred as the headline jumped across my vision: *Fire That Destroyed Mobile Home Possible Arson*

A million pinpricks of pain slammed behind my eyelids, and for the first time all day, the only thing on my mind was whiskey.

I needed the smoky burn of that golden elixir to chase away this bitter taste in my mouth.

I snatched the yellowed newspaper clipping from her hands and quickly skimmed the article.

I remember when my dad had called the *Morning Star* and complained that the sheriff's office wasn't doing a proper investigation.

I pushed my hand through my hair, conjuring the taste of that warm honey liquid that numbed my veins.

"What's that got to do with me?"

"Uh, only *everything*, if I were gonna put money down." She tossed the papers behind her and scooched across the seat, both of her palms coming to rest on the hard line of my jaw. "Will you just talk to me? Drop the tough guy shit and just give me Fallon." Her eyes searched the tired lines of my face. "I know he's still there."

I slammed my eyes closed, wishing with every fiber of my being that the goddamn smell of peaches and honey wasn't invading my nostrils, weakening my walls, shattering me down to the depths of my soul right now.

"You don't know shit about it."

I tossed the milk shake in the garbage can out my window, refusing to meet her eyes while I turned on the engine of the truck.

More I thought about it, the angrier it made me.

The balls she had to waltz in here and start questioning me about my life.

After everything?

I shook my head, wry grin sliding up the corner of my lip as I slid the truck into reverse and backed up, foot heavy on the accelerator.

"Fallon, don't." Her voice was soft, pleading.

I could have used her words that night.

Any words, it didn't matter.

I needed her, and the one time I'd needed her, she wasn't there.

"How long you known about the fire?" I was trying to piece together the timeline in my head.

She looked confused, shaking her head as she thought. "Daddy told me your place had burned down. But not until after college. After I'd moved back home. And I didn't even think about it again until…well, I found the papers."

I let her words hang heavy in the cab, mind tumbling down an exhausting road of what-ifs and whys.

"Guess there's one thing you missed in that article," I finally said.

"What?"

I nodded at the paper settled on the floorboard. "Check the date."

She scrunched her nose, confusion bleeding across her face before she bent, the feathery wisp of paper—the very key—a portal to the worst night of my life. The night that changed everything.

"Says…" Her eyes began the article again. "In the late morning of August fourth, first responders were called to a mobile home off River Ridge Road after neighbors reported a fireball in the distance…" She stopped, tilting her head to one side like a confused little puppy. "August fourth."

"August fourth." My tone hardened with the reminder. "The day *you* disappeared."

TWELVE

Fallon—Ten Years Ago

I pulled the top notebook off a stack of old battered ones and opened it to the last page I'd been working on.

A song.

I'd been tossing the words around in my head for weeks now, my mind obsessing over this single arrangement of notes on my guitar until it finally seemed to be coming together.

I'd been playing around with songwriting since I could remember, a way to express shit I couldn't otherwise articulate. But being with Augusta Belle had kept me so busy I'd hardly had a minute to write anymore.

We spent at least an hour or two together every day, and there were a lot of nights I found myself walking her home, creeping past her passed-out parents and warming myself next to her all night.

I felt like an old dog compared to all the beauty that surrounded her, but I'd grown not to care.

Augusta Belle didn't care about any of that, so why should it bother me if I was holed up in a mobile home on the rougher side of town while she perched like a princess at the top of the ridge?

"Gave my heart to you, was all I had left to lose…" I wrote down a few notes in the lined margin before a familiar tap, tap, tap against my bedroom window jerked me from my thoughts.

"Fallon!"

I dropped my guitar on the floor and threw the window open without a second thought.

"'S'wrong?" I wrapped my arms around Augusta Belle's waist once she'd cleared the single-paned window. "I don't ever lock it, and if you're bold enough to face Chuck Gentry, you probably coulda waltzed through the front door."

"I'm sorry for waking you." Her voice was small, caged inside the emotion in her throat.

"Babe." I hugged her into my chest, instantly alert. "What the fuck happened?"

"They're fighting. It's so bad, I couldn't sleep. I couldn't even hear myself think anymore. I screamed down the stairs at them." She swallowed, eyes brimming over. "I was about to stomp down the stairs and leave right out the front door, but before I could, Mama stomped up the stairs and…" She shook her head, fighting anger and pain. "Mama opened the door and started screaming about me bein' at fault for all their fightin', and then she…" Augusta Belle wiped at her temple, and for the first time, I noticed fresh blood pooling at her hairline.

"Christ, why didn't you say something?" I launched off the bed to retrieve a cool washcloth before she clutched at my T-shirt, her tiny, red-tipped nails glistening in the dim light of the moon.

"Don't leave yet."

Her words slivered my heart in two before I pulled the shirt over my shoulders and balled it up, dabbing it gently at her head to locate and contain the wound.

"Do you think you need stitches?" I asked soberly.

She shook her head, both hands clutching at my forearms then, soft tremors beginning to overtake her body. "Just hold me for a minute."

I swallowed, for the first time feelin' an anger so violent I wanted to drive my truck right up the road and lay into them for hurting their daughter the way they did.

Dimming the light she radiated naturally.

"Worried about you, Augusta Belle. If you'd let me—"

"I'm okay, Fallon. This isn't the first time she's hit me. It's just the first time in a long time."

My eyelids sank closed with the knowledge that something like this had been happening to her right under my nose and I hadn't done anything to stop it.

"You feel dizzy or anything?" I asked, still concerned.

"No." She tucked herself deeper into my body.

I frowned, wishing like hell I could steal her away from that house, from those narcissistic assholes that didn't deserve the special daughter they'd been blessed with. "Wish I could snatch you out of that place."

Her angelic lips turned up at the corners. "I don't need a white knight, Fallon." Her fingers threaded through mine and settled across my bare chest. "This princess saves herself."

I placed a kiss on the dips of her knuckles. "Think of me as the horse you're riding in on, then."

She burst into a soft laugh before stifling it. I pulled another blanket over us, digging deeper into the thin old mattress with the almost see-through sheets.

"Some days I don't know if I'll make it to eighteen alive."

I winced inwardly, thinking not for the first time that she was still the saddest girl I'd ever met.

"You know, I was going to do it that day. I was plannin' it." Her lips brushed against my chest. "You already saved me once."

Augusta Belle's words destroyed me.

Her touch more devastating when our hearts were

shredded raw.

"Save me again," she breathed, her fingertips trailing up my torso before dusting along the stubble at my jaw.

And in that moment, I knew.

I knew there would be no going back for Augusta Belle and me.

"Augusta…" I husked, pleading. For what, I wasn't sure.

"I love you." She peppered kisses along my jaw, sliding her small body on top of mine, all ten fingers lacing together.

I swallowed, feeling like a caged man just given the keys to paradise.

"Love you more, Augusta Belle. But I don't think—"

"Sick of all that thinkin' you're always doin', Fallon Gentry." She brushed her lips against mine and the faint taste of whiskey zapped my senses.

Shit, she'd been drinking. Not like her at all.

"Baby, I want to make sure you're okay."

"I'm so much better now that I'm in your bed." She pushed the sweater over her head, letting it land in a heap on the old linoleum floor before she was pressed to me again. "Only you can make me feel better."

An audible groan escaped my lips as I thought about all the reasons I shouldn't have Augusta Belle in my bed right now.

The second thing that snapped through my brain was

that I probably shouldn't have let things with her get this far to begin with. She was a certain sorta girl, and I really wasn't the type of guy who came from the sorta family that was accepted by people who lived up on the ridge.

"Augusta…" I groaned when her hand began to dance between her thighs, brushing her knuckles against the cotton of my shorts as soft little mewls pranced past her lips. "You're gonna be the death of me."

"I wouldn't have survived without you." She hummed, teeth catching my earlobe just as her hips came down against mine and I realized she was naked. Not a stitch of clothing between her and the cotton of my shorts.

Every bone in my body ached as the thought of really having her made itself real for the first time.

I hadn't let myself go there before.

I didn't think I'd be able to control myself then.

She stroked her heated core against my cock, teeth whispering at the shell of my ear before her hands cupped my cheeks and she pressed a soft kiss to my lips. "I don't want anything between us."

I nodded, blinking once as my palms trailed up her bare torso, the silky flesh of her breasts warm against my rough palms.

She moaned, stroking harder against me before her fingertips were pushing at my waistband.

Something kicked over inside my brain then, a

firestorm of need cascading through me that hurtled us both off the cliff.

In the next instant, she was in my arms and I was pushing her against a wall of my tiny room, my hands shoving down my waistband and finding her hot, warm core radiating against my shaft.

She sucked in a breath of air and moaned, and my jaw clenched down so hard I thought I'd crumble my teeth as I held myself just outside her entrance, hovering, breathing, searing every inch of her to my memory.

"Augusta, I don't have a condom."

Her fingertips worked against the nape of my neck.

"I don't care." She arched, the hot seam of her core scalding my flesh. She pressed her lips and her hips rapidly against mine, lining herself up at precisely the right angle to ease the tip of me just inside her body.

I sucked in a ragged breath, one palm clutching at her thigh as every single moment that didn't include her before this one ceased to exist.

My world tipped, upended itself, and was righted again, spinning at a new rhythm, one that matched her succinctly.

I clamped down my eyelids, burying myself in the wild halo of waves that drowned me in her.

I wouldn't survive this.

I knew it.

I couldn't put my finger on it, but if I thought kinda

sorta saving her on the Whiskey River Bridge that summer day was one meaningful blip in a slow succession of mindless days, then this moment…this was all of it.

Everything good and right in my world culminating right here, in her and me.

Augusta Belle's warm mouth met mine, our tongues igniting in raw desire, our bodies creating chemistry as we connected on a deeper level for the first time.

"I've been waiting my whole life for this." She gulped in a breath of air.

Her words whispering down my neck sent violent pulsations echoing through every nerve.

Buried in her body, everything was heightened, we were so connected.

"I've been waiting all of my life for you."

She clung to me, our bodies swaying together before I pulled her onto the bed, caging her between my arms and tasting every morsel of her sweet existence, losing myself and finding the very best part of me all at once.

There would definitely be no coming back from Augusta Belle Branson. My life from this moment onward could only get sweeter as long as she was in it.

* * *

I woke Augusta Belle in the early morning hours of August fourth. The predawn light just grazing her flushed cheeks as she stirred to life, eyes still drunk with sleep and pleasure. She looked like a woman now, something about her way more grown-up, something that made me proud to call her mine.

I stroked the soft bow of her bottom lip when she finally breathed a quiet good morning. "I never want to leave your arms."

I pulled her to a seated position, bare body clinging to my chest as I worked her shirt over her head and down her arms. "Someday, Augusta Belle. Not today, but soon."

She sighed, stretching each leg out and allowing me to pull the discarded denim up her thighs. "Someday we'll roam the open road like gypsies. You can sing music, and I'll be your dedicated groupie." Her cherub cheeks and innocence were sweet enough to make my jaded heart crack.

"We'll get on that just as soon as you graduate high school." I plopped a chaste kiss on her nose once I'd bundled her up sufficiently.

"That's too long." She scrunched her nose, eyes watering at the edges.

"It'll be over before you know it." I locked our fingers. "In the meantime, I'll keep writing music, you'll keep swimming and breaking records." I pulled the ancient door open and pushed a finger to my lips. "Old man's probably passed out on the couch, but he's a light sleeper some nights."

Two front teeth punctured her bottom lip, and she nodded, eyes trained on me.

I smiled, pulling her a little closer to me and mouthing the words "I love you."

She used sign language to repeat my sentiment, then I pulled her quietly down the hallway and out into the cool morning air.

Our footsteps sped up as the morning light bathed the far-off horizon in a warm glow, dew burning off the tall grass and wetting my sneakers with every step.

We rounded the bend and angled up the steep hill to the top of the ridge.

We'd definitely gotten a late start this morning. She was usually safely tucked in bed by this time of morning, her parents none the wiser that she'd spent the night out. I paused as we reached the first giant hemlock that flanked her driveway.

Her eyes finally locked with mine, and I whispered a kiss across her cheek.

"I may have kinda sorta saved you the first day we met, but…" I breathed another kiss along her temple. "You've been saving me every day since then."

One lonely tear dampened the cotton at my throat, making my own eyes burn with something too strong for either of us to swallow.

"I wish I didn't have to go back there," she finally

squeaked.

I pulled away, squinting away my own tears from the warm dawn light and focusing on the soft skin at her throat. "Where's your necklace?"

Her hand moved to her throat on instinct, searching for the little golden cameo she'd been wearing every moment since I'd given it to her. "It's in my room somewhere. I took it off a few nights ago for a shower and just misplaced it." A frown slid across her face.

"Well, as soon as you find it, put it back on." I pushed a lip between my teeth. "I'd save you again if I could, Augusta Belle." I meant it, every word.

She nodded, trying to control more tears, I could tell.

My eyes glanced up to the still, silent windows of the house at 101 River Ridge Drive.

A bright golden ray cracked through the dappled leaves and kissed the soft waves of her hair.

Her hands finally broke from my grip, and she backed away, moving into the bright sunlight before throwing me an air kiss and a reluctant half smile and then turning to run away with my heart.

I watched her sprint all the way up the driveway before darting around the side of the house where I knew she'd scramble up the old trellis and onto her roof, before sneaking back in through her window and getting ready for her day as if she'd never been gone.

I lingered for a few minutes longer, waiting for what, I

wasn't sure, before I turned and headed back the way I'd come. I retraced my steps back down the ridge and home to my tiny single bed and the worn old quilt that'd kept me warm since I was a kid. Except this time, it smelled like Augusta Belle.

My footsteps sped up as I rounded the last corner and darted across the small yard and through the front door of my home.

"Up early this morning, son." Dad's whiskey-clogged voice rang in my ears.

"Went for a jog. It's gonna be a beautiful day." I clapped the old man on the back, glad to see he was at least up and off the couch, a rarity this time of day.

Nerve pain usually kept his body so buckled and bent he could hardly make it off the couch. That'd been part of the reason I'd moved to Chickasaw Ridge. To help him. The other because my mama had found herself doing another ninety-day stint in rehab, and I just couldn't make the bills on our small rental alone.

"Sure is a beautiful day, son. Sure is." He took a long drink of water as he stood at the kitchen sink that overlooked the field and ridge beyond. One of his hands clutched at the chipped countertop, hip twisted to one side as he favored some painful ache.

"Don't forget to take your vitamins this morning. 'Kay, dad?"

He nodded once, an indulgent grin spreading his thin

lips.

"I'm gonna hop in the shower then take the Jeep into town. I have a friend I think might be able to fix that radiator for cheap…" My words hung heavy in the air when I noticed something else had caught the old man's attention, and he was shuffling back to his semi-permanent placement on the couch.

I shook my head, vowing to stop by the VFW on my way into town and see if any of the old guys would be willing to come out and visit my dad a few times a week. I also wanted to ask if any of them had a lead on some construction jobs. The few gigs I was getting in town weren't near enough to pay for dinner, much less anything else.

It was hard for me to keep regular hours when I was helping my dad so much of the day, but my sister had promised to start stopping after work a few days a week to check on him if I found regular work.

If I was going to make a life with Augusta, I'd have to start lining up my cards early.

I had less than a year to make sure my dad could and would be good on his own in this place if I had any chance of getting Augusta Belle out of hers. I didn't have much saved, but between what I did have and a full-time job, plus singing for tips on weekends, I figured I could afford to keep a roof over our heads while she went to college. I'd already decided wherever she wanted to go, I was game. From LA to New York, and anywhere in between.

I was stepping out of the shower not much later when the idling of a car engine caught my attention.

I cracked the old crank window in the bathroom, wincing when the rusted hinges protested, before a flaming orange ball of light crossed my vision.

The sound of shattering glass splintered my senses a moment later, a little dark car spinning off around the corner and up the hill.

Adrenaline pummeled my body as I pulled on my dirty clothes and launched out the door and down the hallway.

Fire engulfed the kitchen, a bottle with a heavy white rag still rocking on the linoleum floor as pieces of the faded flower tile melted around it.

My muscles tensed as I saw my father cast sideways on a couch that was already quickly becoming swallowed in flames.

I breathed into my T-shirt and tried to remember where Dad kept the fire extinguisher.

I gnashed down on my teeth, realizing I didn't have time for that before I launched across the living room and pulled the heavy weight of my father through the front door.

I heaved in fresh lungfuls of air as his face turned a worrisome ashen color.

I looked back up at the house, seeing flames lick out the window now, realizing I could either start CPR on my father, or run back into that trailer and hope to find my phone in my bedroom to call the fire department.

I didn't have time for both.

I looked up at the sky, eyes watering from the smoke now cascading out of every window of our trailer.

If I thought I knew devastation before, it was dim in comparison to what was about to come next.

The darkest days of my life, creeping by one agonizing instant at a time as we tried to recover, as I tried to rebuild. Just when everything was fallin' apart.

THIRTEEN

Fallon

"I didn't disappear." Her eyes welled up with tears, one salted track trailing over the arch of her cheekbone. "That's not…" More tears started to flow, her voice choked with emotion. "If you only knew what happened when you left me on the road that day."

Her words battered my heart with their raw pain. "Christ, don't cry, Augusta Belle."

I groaned, pulling over into the first parking lot I found, a hotel chain I'd stayed with a few times in the past. "Could never stand it when you started crying. And I didn't just leave you on the road."

I slid her over the seat toward me, her tears growing stronger as I enveloped her quaking form in my arms. "I wish I was there for you that night, Fallon, more than

100

anything, but I can't go back in time and change it. And trust me when I say I'd rather be with you any day than where I was…"

I shook my head, not even giving a shit anymore about the years of hardship that had fallen on my shoulders, all beginning with that night.

I'd moved to Chickasaw Ridge to help my dad. The irony was that by the time I left, he was already in the ground, that little burned trailer hauled off to the junkyard, every piece of evidence of my life in Chickasaw along with it.

"If I would have known that happened… Well, if I could have come back, I would have. You know that, right, Fallon?" Her brandy eyes gazed up at me, pleading for some sort of absolution I didn't know I had it in me to give.

"That was a long time ago." I pushed a hand through my too-long hair, breathing a sigh of relief when she scooted back across the bench seat and took to gazin' out the window.

The miles of open road rolled by in silence after that. Hours of thoughts hanging heavy between us, neither one of us brave enough to bring a voice to the things we'd been waiting a decade to say.

I'd had different words on the tip of my tongue a dozen times, and then I'd sneak a glance at her, looking all lonely and lost in her thoughts. And for the first time in nearly a fucking decade, I wondered what in the hell it'd been that I was chasing out here.

For so long, I'd run from town to town following some lofty idea that I might find her again.

And then I'd resigned myself to the fact that she was gone forever.

And then finally, I'd decided that everything she'd done, she'd done with the sole purpose of tearing my fucking heart out and burying it in the cold country clay under her feet.

Truth be told, none of those estimations was quite right, and havin' her here turned every damn thing I thought I was thinking upside down.

We were passing the "Welcome to Memphis" sign a dozen miles later when I punched the address of the little dive bar into my navigation system and followed the route to Slick Willy's.

I grinned when we pulled up alongside the little establishment, so small they probably couldn't pack in more than a hundred folks at a time. I could smell the burn of cheap whiskey already.

"Looks like this is home the next few nights," I said aloud before realizing she was with me and I had promised to boot her once we got to Memphis.

And now here we were. Only thing was, she was huddled up over there looking so sad and broken.

I suppressed a groan before I took in our

surroundings. A chain hotel perched just down the street looked clean enough for my needs.

I steered the truck in that direction, then shifted into park and paused, lingering at the door handle as I wondered whether or not to say anything before I went to the reservation desk.

I shook my head silently, opting to leave her to her thoughts.

I'd had a damn decade to get used to the fact that my life had changed irreparably that night, that I'd soon found myself as the sole caregiver for a man in rapidly failing health, that the girl I'd sworn my whole heart to had vanished without a trace. That the fire that'd taken so much away from me may have been an act of arson.

The fact that Augusta Belle wasn't there for any of it was inconsequential to me at this point.

I'd had to get along regardless, and I hadn't done a half-bad job, whiskey bottle aside.

I stepped out of the hotel's main office fifteen minutes later with two keycards in hand, a healthy drizzle now coating my windshield, and Augusta Belle still curled peacefully in the passenger seat, just like I'd left her.

My eyes quickly registered an Italian pizzeria joint across the street, with a liquor store right beside it.

Memphis catered to all my essentials.

I frowned. The familiar warmth of that smoky aroma curling around my nostrils as I opened a bottle of Jack for the first time had me fightin' to keep myself in line. Cravings tore through my veins as the need to soak myself in liquor reared it's ugly head.

I swallowed the memory of warmth washing my insides, heart ratcheting up to a gallop as the neon lights across the street called to me.

I chomped down on my bottom lip, struggling for any sense of control to keep me planted in the present, when a clap of thunder echoed across the sky.

My eyes cut across the lot to Augusta.

The only thing stopping me from walking through that liquor store's swingin' door was the little girl perched in my front seat, not a soul left on this earth to love her but me.

I grunted to myself, uncomfortable with the idea of anyone at all relyin' on me and leaving a pit of something like dread deep in my stomach. But I didn't think about that, just trudged on across the street, eyes trained on the homemade pizza that would soon be in my future.

I was walking back across the street a handful of minutes later with a warm pie in my hands when I approached my truck to find Augusta Belle perched on the seat, passenger door open and a bottle of booze between her thighs.

"Christ," I muttered under my breath as she took a slow swig with her lips, throat contracting in numerous swallows.

The way she was hugging my best stuff made me think she'd been doin' this a lot of nights, but that wasn't any of my business. In fact, nothin' about her was. I was just doing my duty to humanity, making sure she was fed and had a roof over her head.

"Pizza, party for two?" I flipped her the keycards in my palm, and she snagged one, pulling her backpack over one shoulder and tucking the whiskey bottle under her armpit before we pushed through the double doors of the hotel and headed for the third-floor room.

"I told them two beds," I said when she was pushing in the door of the room a minute later.

She didn't say a word, only threw her black backpack on the bed, flopping down onto it herself before uncapping the whiskey and taking another swig.

"That's bad ya, know. Some old-timer gave it to me after a show once. Called it white lightnin'." I tossed the pizza on the counter and kicked off my boots by the front door. "Can't promise you're safe drinkin' it."

She only shrugged, pushing the whiskey bottle on the faux-wood tabletop, eyes dragging across the room before landing on mine.

That look didn't promise anything good.

"Y'know, you think you're so innocent in this, just walking away like you did. Turnin' into a big star in Nashville, dating those pop star twits." She pushed a hand through the air as if to wave away the irritating flies. "I was all alone."

She hiccupped, frustrated tears hovering at her eyelashes.

I wanted nothing more than to lick away her pain, take it all from her until the only thing left standing was her and me and that special thing we had together.

"We've gotta be at the gig in two hours. Think you're gonna be ready, champ? Or you sittin' this one out?"

Her eyes shot open but refused to focus. "I'm totally fine. Besides, m'not going to your show anyway. I'm just gonna take a shower then find the nearest bus station and head back to the Ridge." She stood from the bed, pulling her shirt over her head and stumbling slowly to the bathroom.

"That's the closet, actually." I spoke up when she opened the wrong door.

I guided her into the bathroom before turning on the hot-water tap.

"I'll be back in to check on you." I placed a kiss on the furrow of her forehead.

"Don't need your saving, Gentry."

"I know you don't, Branson. Never did," I offered, retreating back out the door and closing it softly in my wake.

I slumped down on the office chair, pushing cooling box of pizza aside and looking longingly across the room at that golden liquid belonging to me.

I hadn't expected her to be the one to hit the bottle, but some truths were just too destructive to bear without some liquid courage, I supposed.

And hell if I was anyone to judge.

A few new lines to the song I'd been working on materialized in my mind, and I scratched out some words on a stray pad of paper and hotel-logoed pen. *I've got this monkey on my back…these habits I can't break… You left me here standing in the early dawn light, and all I got is more pain…*

I heard the steady hum of the shower through the thin wooden door as I fell further into the song, matching some of the words to notes I could imagine playing under my fingers. In a few more weeks, this could be ready to sing onstage. I'd written hundreds of songs in just the same way in the years I'd been on the road.

Seems Augusta Belle disappearin' had worked wonders for my creative side.

I scratched out a couple more notes about the arrangement of the music, and before long, the water in the shower was kicking off and the door squeaking open.

"Thanks," she hummed, honey silk ringlets falling around her ivory shoulders, a fluffy white towel wrapped around her body.

She looked so fragile, like a rare bird that needed extra-gentle handling.

"I'm not sure what got into me." She avoided my eyes and went to the bed, shuffling through the backpack before pausing, clean change of clothes in her hands.

She chomped down on her lip, taking a few tentative steps closer to me. "I know I just showed up in your life like a ghost out of thin air…"

"Took the thoughts out of my head," I affirmed.

"And I know you don't have to put up with me." She hardly suppressed an eye roll, the admission painful for her still-stubborn self. "But I appreciate it." She paused as if considering whether or not to say more. She seemed to decide against it before adding, "I would love to see your show tonight."

And then she disappeared back into the bathroom, a cloud of spiced peaches and smoky whiskey leaving a dreamy, numbing warmth in her wake.

FOURTEEN

Fallon

I sauntered through the door of Slick Willy's later that night, Augusta Belle hot on my heels, her hand wrapped firmly in mine.

Something had shifted after our moment in the truck earlier.

I couldn't put my finger on exactly what it was, but she seemed a little more raw, like she'd been stripped of a few of her shields of armor, and I couldn't help bein' a little more tender to that.

I still had questions.

Plenty of emotions, too, but they didn't seem as important to me as they once were.

There was no changin' the past, so I was doin' my best to live in each moment.

And in this moment, I had her.

"Fallon Gentry here for eight," I said when we'd landed at the bar.

The man nodded toward the corner of the room. A tiny stage barely big enough for one sat waiting, a few dozen scattered chairs and hardly anyone in sight.

"You bother promotin' this?"

"Not my job." He shrugged. "Didn't think Nashville's golden boy needed promotin' anyway. Heard you packed the Thorny Cactus. Didn't figure I needed to—"

I didn't wait for the rest of his bullshit excuse, only trailed my way among the litter of chairs to get to the stage. "Most of these places have at least a room in back to warm up, but looks like we're goin' in cold tonight. Got anything you know off the top of your head?"

"Me?" Augusta Belle dropped my hand and backed away a few steps, head shaking. "I'm not singin' tonight. I haven't sung in years."

"So? Still got the pipes, don't ya?"

She tilted her head, eyes flaring, and I knew then she'd accepted my challenge.

"I got you, slick." She narrowed her gaze, pushing past me to step up onstage and adjust the microphone to her height. "You ready?"

One of her eyebrows quirked up. Check. Mate.

"Born ready." I stepped up beside her and waited as she hummed a few notes into the microphone, eyes darting up to meet mine when a few customers wandered over and took seats.

She had that look in her eye that said she wasn't sure if she was going to sing her ass off or puke her guts out, that very feeling I lived for—when adrenaline and whiskey mixed—a ride-or-die moment.

Her sweet Southern twang was music to my ears as she sang the opening lines of a June Carter and Johnny Cash song, words about getting married in a wild fever rush.

My heart throttled into a gallop as my fingers took over the familiar notes of the song, her perfect harmonies mixing with the words to create some special blend of magic in that dingy little bar.

I sang my part when it came, her eyes hovering on mine as we turned, singing back and forth about love and pain and all the crazy that comes along with walkin' hand in hand with someone an entire lifetime.

By the time the song had finished, the tiny bar was nearly packed, new people still coming in off the street as the energy hit record decibels.

I winked at Augusta Belle as the song ended and led her into the next song I knew she'd remember.

A song I'd sung to her more nights than I could count.

I couldn't let myself think about all the sweet and tender moments of our growing up together, culminating in the night when it was all ripped away from us. I couldn't think about it, or I'd find myself breaking down on this stage right here and now and askin' her to give me everything.

All that heartache had made me think some hateful things, the only absolution I could find at the bottom of a dry whiskey bottle.

I wasn't any different from a lot of the men who loved strong women. That independent fire was what drew me to her, but it also had to keep me ready to let her fly, when that time came.

By the time we'd finished our third song in a row, the crowd was standing room only.

Augusta Belle's face was lit from ear to ear for the first time since I'd finally set eyes on her sweet self again, and I was just the intoxicated asshole sitting on the sidelines, happy to be in the glow of her sunlight.

It'd been a long damn time since I'd felt the shine of the sun on my face.

I set my guitar down for a moment, reaching for the bottle of beer the bartender had deposited at the side of the stage for me.

A few soft strums of an familiar tune about rendered me speechless.

I spun, eyes focused on my girl, sitting center stage on the stool, my old guitar in her lap.

Her voice, clear and sweeter than a blackbird, echoed through the small room, now standing silently, watching her.

I stepped off the stage, watching them watch her as she crooned the sweet melody of an old Beatles song.

Something inside cracked my heart open, watching her perform up there all by herself.

I couldn't help thinking how natural she looked.

And where she'd learned to play guitar like that, I couldn't fathom. She'd only had a basic understanding with a few simple songs I'd taught her before…well, that night.

I gnawed on my bottom lip, feeling the muscles in my body relax one by one as she opened up to the song, sang it slow and sweet, drawing out the end notes like an angel.

How I'd survived without her all these years, I didn't know.

I certainly hadn't done a very good job of it. Just a day spent with her proved it.

I sighed, something deep rooting down inside me as she ended the song on a quiet note, then hung her head, eyes casting up at me through her eyelashes with a hesitant smile.

I was so fucking proud of her I wanted to scoop her into my arms and take her back to that hotel room right now.

My rare bird, always poised on the edge, finally ready to fly.

I pushed a hand through my hair, stepping up onstage and passing her the cold beer.

She took a slow sip, then passed my guitar back to me.

I grinned recklessly, a downright happy feeling coming over me for the first time in too long.

"Got any more surprises?" I crooked a grin.

She shrugged one shoulder, the mischievous glint in her eye telling me all I needed to know.

I licked my lips, sliding the other stool up beside her, cradling my guitar in my lap and strumming the first few notes to a song I knew everyone would know.

"Whiskey Girl."

I'd been dreading performing this one in front of her, certainly hadn't planned on her being shoulder to shoulder with me when I did.

But I carried on, gave the people the one song they could all sing along to. *"It's not easy to forget, the bitter taste lovin' you left…"*

I caught a glimpse of Augusta Belle, still at my side as I sang the song, tore my soul open, and laid it at her feet.

I'd written this song in the first week she'd been gone, hadn't even intended for another soul to hear it.

And now here I was, sharing my rawest pain with not just the entire world, but the girl who'd inspired it.

"Always my favorite sin, even when I swore I wouldn't go back again…"

I held the middle chorus, stretching out the sweet,

haunting notes of the guitar longer than they were all used to, something I'd been playin' with over the last few months. It gave the song more of a "Hotel California" feeling, forlorn and regretful.

It'd matched my state of mind then, but now that she was here, shining her impossibly bright light all over my life, I could help but think it was too much, a wallowing in the pain that was no longer necessary.

I jumped into the final chorus, when the speed picked up and ended on the rousing anthem everyone expected. *"Lookin' for love in the same ole places…"*

I ended, for the first time in three and a half minutes forgetting she was hovering at my side.

I cast a glance her way just as the audience erupted into a spray of clapping.

Augusta Belle was wiping at a tear, face racked with so much emotion it felt like I'd laid her wide open for the world to inspect along with me.

I didn't know what I'd thought, having her come onstage with me tonight. Didn't know what she thought either, but I should have known better. This world was too mean for a girl like her. Hell, it was too mean for a guy like me.

I didn't know if I'd end up regretting this night, but I definitely knew it made me feel at home for the first time in all these years on the road. And that was a feeling that'd been long lost on me.

By the time I'd managed to wrest Augusta Belle away from the crowd and out into the cool night, I pulled her hand in mine, hauling her across the small space that separated us. "You doin' okay?"

Her eyes cast up, moonlight shimmering off her whiskey-rimmed irises. "That song… The way you sang it." A small shiver raced through her body. "It's like it brought back everything."

The way her voice cracked on the last word—*everything*—had my own heart fallin' between my boots.

I pushed a hand through my hair, adjusting the guitar on my back before throwing an arm over her shoulder and pulling her into my space. Right where I liked her.

"We've been through a lot," I admitted softly, nose brushing against the corn-silk wisps of her hair. "Just sorry I shared it with the world is all."

She shook her head, wiping at another tear. "It's not that. I'm glad you shared it. You went through so much after I was gone…"

Her steps slowed, body reduced to near tremors as she held her face in her hand and finally let the tears pour.

I enveloped her in my arms, wishing I could take away every ounce of this pain splitting her in two right now.

I'd spent so many years wishin' for this day to come, I hadn't stopped to think about what it'd be like if it actually did.

Hell.

Reliving our pasts together felt like a living hell.

Except, before I had whiskey. Now I was too hell-bent on makin' sure she was okay to even think about the crutch that'd been my constant companion for so many years.

"I missed singing with you, even if I'm not very good," she offered, trying to lighten the situation.

"You were born to fly, Augusta Belle." I brushed her silky, damp skin with the pad of my thumb. "Some people never get beyond fearin' the fall. But never forget that you, my dear, were born with just enough rebel heart to leap and *soar*."

Her eyes filled with water all over again, raw emotion spilling over as a soft drizzle of rain somehow wiped away the things clinging to both of us.

"I missed this." I paused, letting the rain mist around us. "I missed *us.*"

Before my mind could register a single opinion about it, I ducked my head, pushing my lips softly against hers.

Honey and peaches.

The only thing I could think in the few milliseconds my lips brushed hers was that she still tasted like honey and peaches.

I pulled away, heart clawing its way out of my throat, the burn seared by her lips on mine still sending tingles through my veins.

I interrupted the awkward silence with a soft groan,

looking up at the sky just as heavy raindrops began falling.

My fingers ached to slide into hers again, dig my nose into her hair and make sure she was safe from any sorta pain that might be coming, but I couldn't.

I wasn't ready.

Our history may have been long buried in the past, but there was a lot of it.

Augusta Belle's wet fingers threaded through my own then, resting her head on my shoulder. "Let's go inside, Fallon."

I swallowed the jagged shards clogging my throat before nodding, taking a moment to place a kiss on her damp forehead before leading her through the double doors of the hotel and up to our room.

As soon as I swung the door open, Augusta was kicking off her shoes and moving across the carpet, eyes on the pillows. She curled up in bed, losing herself in the mountain of covers before peeking out, her silky dark eyes swimming up at me as a soft smile parted her lips. "Thanks for letting me sing with you." Her grin deepened. "I loved it. I'm surprised how much I loved it. I didn't even think, I just started singin' like I always do."

I sat next to her on the bed, back propped against the headboard, the fingertips of one hand tracing through the waves of her hair. "Surprised me, I'll give ya that."

"Didn't think I could sing?" She curled against my

torso, one arm draping across my chest.

"Oh, I knew you could sing. Just didn't think you could do it onstage." I paused, remembering the feeling of seeing her up there, singin' her sweet heart out like a songbird. "Hell, most days I don't want to do it, but you looked natural."

Her teeth clamped down on her bottom lip, eyes fading somewhere far away. "Does that mean you're gonna let me stay and sing with you tomorrow?"

I couldn't help but smile. "Lookin' forward to it."

She paused, fingertips drawing invisible circles around the cotton of my T-shirt before she finally said, "I hated 'Whiskey Girl' when it first came on the radio."

I barked a laugh before stifling it with the back of my hand and replying, "S'that right?"

"Oh. Yeah." She emphasized both words. "When everyone was singing it on their smuggled MP3 players, I wanted to strangle them each with the headphone cord." Her eyes fell closed, tense muscles of her angelic face softening. "Then they told me the name of the singer. Fallon Gentry." She yawned, snuggling a little deeper into my arms. "And then I knew why I hated it. It was about us. I didn't even wanna come home to the Ridge after that. Mama said the rumor mill was workin' overtime." Her voice grew quiet, a little sadder. "I just couldn't face it all over again."

I nodded, for the first time understanding the position

I'd put her in when I'd signed off on the worldwide release of "Whiskey Girl" to those producers. It'd never been about me. That song was about both of us.

And maybe deep down, even then, I'd known that, and that's why I'd done it anyway. A misplaced sense of revenge. Or maybe a beacon. Probably both.

Augusta Belle sniffed softly, lips parting as her breaths found a slower rhythm.

My eyes cast around the room, taking in the small place, the lonely bottle of amber liquid the only thing glinting in the silver moonlight.

I groaned, adjusting myself around her slightly, the idea of waking her up at all preventing me from doing anything more.

I licked my lips, mouth watering as I thought about just a small nightcap to put me to sleep.

And then Augusta Belle sighed in her sleep, remindin' me that right here with her in my arms I was a helluva lot better than I'd been in a while. I licked my lips, mind wandering to that song I'd been working over in my head.

"Wait. Smuggled MP3 players?" My brain finally settled on the new bit of information she'd mentioned. "Where the hell *were* you, Augusta?"

But by that time, her eyes were already drifting closed, shallow breaths deepening.

I stifled a groan, wondering where in the hell she

could have been hiding out ten years ago.

I pushed myself down deeper into the duvet, turning over to wrap Augusta Belle in my arms fully.

A brief smile turned her lips before she breathed sweetly, "I love you, Fallon."

I fell asleep that night with a heart the size of eastern Tennessee thrumming in my chest, my soul finally quiet now that it'd found its mate again.

Even if the sweet honey scent of her left an afterburn I wasn't yet willing to brave.

FIFTEEN

Fallon

I woke up the next morning, the smell of peaches and honey absent.

My eyes shot open, and I pulled myself out of the bed, my only thought on finding Augusta.

I listened for a quiet moment, eyes drawn to the bathroom door when a soft humming came from that area. I walked across the room, grin pulling up my lips when I caught sight of her, hair piled into a messy bun on the top of her head, a notebook propped on one damp knee as she scratched notes with a pencil.

"Mornin'." I breathed, stepping a little farther into the room.

Her gaze lit up when our eyes connected, and she held the notebook to her chest, the papers blotted with soapy wet spots from the bathwater, but she didn't seem to care. "I've been writing."

"Oh?" I sat on the edge of the tub. "Can I?"

She held out the notebook, sinking a little deeper under the soapy bubbles as her cheeks pinked up with the heat in the room.

My eyes scanned the scribbled notes, stanzas and lines strewn across the page.

I nodded my head, humming along a melody to a few of the lines before peeking up at her over the spiral pages and grinning. "This is good."

"Really?" She smiled with some small sense of disbelief.

"Really." I flipped a page, and then another, then three more in a row after that. "How many of these notebooks do you have?"

"A lot. I kept all of them. I have an entire box at home too. Writing made me feel—" her eyes flicked up to the ceiling as she shrugged "—closer to you."

She stole the breath from my lungs with her admission.

Was it really possible that I'd been on her mind all of the last decade just like she'd been on mine?

Losing you was the final nail, the last piece of us, buryin' my coffin…

I could definitely appreciate her Southern sound, but I didn't know if she was ready to sing these lyrics every night. And hell if I was ready to hear them.

"We should put some of them to music." I found myself saying the exact opposite of what I was thinking, but only because not doing it would be an injustice. I knew better than anyone that makin' music was a matter of layin' your soul on the page for all to see. There was somethin' therapeutic about writin' things down. No way would I take that away from her.

"There's this certain arrangement that I think would sound so good paired with these words." She leaned farther out of the tub, swiping the notebook and flipping through the pages.

And that was how I found myself fallin' for Augusta Belle again.

Slow and steady, one beat at a time, mostly to the sound of music.

I don't know what I was thinking when she proposed later that morning that I needed a haircut.

She looked so cute sittin' across from me, notebook on one knee, my guitar perched over the other, I didn't have the heart to deny her.

I grunted, shoving a hand through my hair and thinking it was getting on my nerves anyway. "S'pose it's about time."

A wicked grin turned up her cheeks before she set my guitar on the bed and rummaged through her makeup bag, pulling out a pair of scissors and heading back for me.

"Wait, you're gonna do it?" I widened my eyes.

"Bet your sweet ass I am."

I was about to steal those scissors right out of her determined little fist, but I burst into a laugh instead.

She grinned, sidling up close before straddling my lap and plopping down on my thighs.

I stifled another strangled moan of frustration, the tiny little shorts she wore doing nothing to help me contain my growing need.

"Just a few inches." That bewitching smile did something to me, something I didn't even like to think about.

"Fine, but don't forget we've got a show tonight. Got to impress the people at Slick Willy's."

She stuck out her tongue, wiggling and shifting around for a second before her fingers stroked through the too-long licks of my dark hair.

She sucked her lips between her teeth as her gaze focused on the ends, sliding them between her fingers before she snipped off the first bit.

I had to close my eyes for the rest.

"Did'ju get a degree in hair-cuttin' over the last ten by any chance?" I asked when she was still snipping a few minutes later.

She shook her head, lips still clamped together as she concentrated on each tiny cut.

Sweet Jesus, I was regretting this decision already.

A second later, she seemed to be finished, tugging on my beard for a brief moment before she took to trimming that with her little scissors from hell.

I nearly stopped her, clasped on to her dainty little wrist and everything. "Good girls don't touch the beard without askin'."

Her eyes widened, a devilish glint lighting her eyes before she pursed her lips and purred, "Now who said anything 'bout bein' good?" Her flirty eyes locked with mine. "Your beard needs a trim, Fallon. Do you mind?"

I narrowed my eyes, assessing her seriously before lowering my hand in defeat. "Some old guy a few towns ago told me I acted too damn old for my age."

She paused, scissors hovering just out of the line of fire. "And you think that may be about the beard?"

I shrugged, thinking it as possible as anything else.

"Well, I don't think it was necessarily the wild thing you've been growing on your face that he was talkin' about. But trimmin' it up a little would probably be a good start to losing that—" she tipped her head to one side "—hobo thing you've got going on."

I pushed a hand through my beard, frowning once before deciding to explain its existence a little more. "Started growing the beard the day I left Nashville." I averted my eyes out the window, rain droplet tracking down the pane. "Figured it was a good way to disguise my face after…everything."

"Everything," she breathed, snipping away at the edges of my beard. "Does everything include that fling you had with Tanner Smith?"

I couldn't help the eye roll then, picking Augusta Belle up off my lap and depositing her on her feet before stalking off into the bathroom to wash the whiskers from my face.

"And?" She cocked her hip against the doorframe, watching me intently in the mirror.

"You knew about that from…wherever you were?" I attempted to deflect, but she wasn't having it.

"When Nashville's biggest star has a high-profile relationship with Hollywood's next It Girl, it gets around."

My face tilted up at the memory.

It had looked pretty bad from the outside.

"You understand where the beard comes in, then?"

She shook her head, walking slowly to me. "No, not really."

"Well, the thing about Tanner and me… The label wanted to put us together on a single. They set up a few meetings, a dinner, and every damn time we were together, the press was always there. Every time. I didn't think much about it then. I was new, thought it was normal, but then the press started running these headlines about Tanner and me dating. And we weren't at all. It was strictly business." I turned, sliding a hand around her shoulders and pulling her a little closer to me. "I was still so hung up on you I couldn't think straight." I gnashed my teeth, thinking if she'd never gone away, none of this would have had a chance to happen. "I tried to get the label to squash the rumors, but it wasn't long before I realized they were flaming them, calling in the fucking paparazzi to make sure we were tomorrow morning's Page Six news.

"That's why I left the industry. Couldn't stand it anymore. It wasn't about the music. It was about the money."

Augusta Belle wrapped her arms around me in the biggest hug her little arms could manage. "I'm sorry it wasn't what you wanted it to be."

I swallowed the familiar old burn of Nashville, pushing the bitterness aside for something brighter. "But I'm happy as hell now. Livin' on the road is where I'm meant to be. Performin' small rooms, meetin' the people who come out to see me."

"Yeah, but still, kinda sucks. Everyone wants to make it big in Nashville, and you did, but then you got there…" She shook her head, empathy coloring every feature. "I mean, who needs Nashville at all? You just need a recording studio, a little money put together, and get a band and some equipment."

"Not really room for that in the cab of my truck."

She threaded her fingers with mine. "Maybe not there. You could do it out of the house in Chickasaw Ridge." She squeezed my hand, hopeful.

"Ain't goin' back there. Besides, said yourself you want to put it up for sale."

"I do," she said thoughtfully, "but you've got options now."

We stayed like that, long minutes stretching in silence until she was curled on my lap and we were sitting in front of the windows streaked with rain.

"Y'know, rainy days aren't so bad when they're with you."

She wrapped both of her arms around my torso, fingertips itching under the soft denim waistband of my worn blue jeans. "All of my best days have been with you."

I rubbed a flat palm over the curves of her spine, wishing things for both of us had been different.

But they weren't, and we were left dealing with the consequences.

The knowledge that Augusta Belle was my salvation wasn't a new one. The realization that maybe even now I still needed her in my life more than she needed me burned like a cheap rye lighting a trail of fire down my throat.

We had a lot to atone for, Augusta Belle and me.

Maybe too much.

SIXTEEN

Fallon

Augusta Belle's whiskey-brown eyes held mine, her lips turning into a sweet half smile before she sang the same opening lines that'd fired up the same crowd at Slick Willy's last night, the bar packed to over-capacity tonight.

It was true what they said. News travels fast in a small town, and apparently, today's news was the reunion of Fallon Gentry and his whiskey girl.

People'd asked both of us to pose for pictures as we'd made our way in through the packed crowd, glasses of whiskey offered to each of us from every other outstretched hand.

I was thankful as fuck I didn't look like the guy who was smiling weakly on the cover of that single they were thrusting at me. That guy wasn't me. Never was. The man I was now might be a little rougher around the edges, but he was a helluva lot wiser and a lot more confident than he had been.

I'd earned this scowl, dammit.

It wasn't until Augusta Belle crooned the opening lines of "Jackson" that my scowl lifted at the edges, my instincts to sing kicking in as we fell into a perfect harmony, arguing in lyrics and having fun every word of the way. Something about this song made me happy, everything about Augusta Belle made me *me*.

By the time we'd breezed through six more songs together, I finally sat center stage and gave them the one song they'd all come for.

The one that'd been a thorn in my side, that I'd been dreading as we'd inched closer to it every minute of tonight.

I started the opening lines, twisting the notes a little to add a quicker tempo, something the crowd didn't recognize immediately. Not until I began with the opening lines: *It's not easy to forget, the bitter taste lovin' you left…*

A few women in the room sighed, the crowd hushing as a short gasp spread through the noise.

I charged on, sticking with the kickier tempo, the one they might not have been used to but the one that felt more like me.

The me now, anyway.

The me not soaked in whiskey and hell-bent on bitterness.

I slowed down a few words of the final chorus, my eyes finally brave enough to chance a glance at Augusta.

She was standing riveted off stage, both hands clasped over her mouth, eyes wide with tears, but also with something else. Pride, maybe.

I winked at her once, voice slipping into the last haunting lyric of the song before I let my guitar end on a soft note and stood, ducking into the darkness of backstage as the crowd erupted into a fit of applause.

Adrenaline charging through my veins, I clasped Augusta's fingers, guiding her quickly through the back hallway and into the fresh air.

She squealed, spinning me around and leaping into my arms.

I yelled into her hair, a smile spreading across my lips, the widest I'd had since I didn't know when.

"That was fucking incredible!" Her breath was hot on my neck, lips hovering just out of reach of mine.

I let her slide down my body, her feet landing on the pavement before we locked fingers and walked off down the sidewalk, getting lost in the crowds of a busy Memphis night.

"Now will you let me do a few gigs with you? I promise I won't get in the way." The moonlight lit her cheekbones, shadows dancing across the soft planes and making me feel some sort of way I couldn't quite put my finger on.

Did I like spending time with Augusta Belle again?

Sure.

Did I want to do it every day?

I worked that thought over in my mind, so many questions still hanging like a cloud over us, lightning and thunder just waitin' to erupt.

"Sure that's what you want?" I asked finally.

Her shoulder brushed side by side with mine, late summer air still thick with humidity, suffocating us like a blanket charged with electricity.

"I've never been more sure of anything."

I faltered a step, a bitter taste rising up the back of my throat as I thought about all the things left unsaid. "We still got a lot that needs sayin' between us, Augusta."

She nodded, eyes casting up to the dark sky as emotions tore across the features of her face. "Do you think…" She pressed her fists together, twisting the fingers and looking everywhere but at me in that moment. "Will it ever be possible for us to start over? So much was stolen from us, all of it out of our control. When it was just you and me makin' the decisions, we were good. We were always so good." She reached out a hand, brushing my forearm.

I couldn't help the hardened pain that'd begun

135

glossing my eyes. "Been through a lot, Augusta Belle, and I've been open, like a fucking book, for every question you've had. There's still a big question mark in my head, though. There's one thing you still haven't answered, and maybe that's because you're not ready, or you think I don't want to hear it." I shook my head, jaw working back and forth as so many fucking memories slid in and out of my brain. "It's been real nice living in this little bubble of sunshine the last few days with you, but that's not reality. That's still running away. And now you're askin' me if we can start over? If we can just be us again? After everything?" I shook my head, attempting and failing to process all the contradictory feelings running through me. "I don't think it works like that."

Her eyes downcast, she frowned, leaning against the tailgate of my truck, arms crossed as she seemed lost in her own mess of feelings.

"I don't wanna stay another night in this shithole," I said, eyes taking in the run-down three-story hotel we'd been in the last two nights. "I wanna get on the road to Tupelo tonight. Pack up your shit, and we can talk more about it in the truck." I pushed a hand through my hair. The memory of her perched on my lap, snuggled up against me and invading my space just this morning as she cut my hair and trimmed my beard almost felt like a dream. "Or," I finally breathed my last offer, "I can get you a ticket home."

She swallowed, eyes crossing the expanse separating us. "Last time I was in Mississippi, I was eighteen."

Her words hung heavy in the air, pregnant with some hidden meaning.

I'd been with her for her sixteenth and seventeenth birthdays, but she would have turned eighteen after…

I cleared my throat, stepping closer to her, resting a palm on her arm because not touching her was becoming too much to bear. "You were in Mississippi?"

She nodded, body beginning to tremble softly as her mind seemed to shift back to a time a decade earlier. "You don't think I'm ready to face the past? But what if you're not, Fallon?"

I screwed my eyes up, surprised by the strength lacing her voice when she looked like a broken little bird in front of me now. "What happened between the time I brought you home and your eighteenth birthday, Augusta Belle?" I held both of her shoulders in my hands, ducking down to her level, desperate for the goddamned closure I'd been denied for so long. "Not knowin' what happened to you…" I swallowed the painful baseball in my throat. "It about killed me."

"You want to know what happened after I climbed through my bedroom window that day?" She narrowed her eyes. "Absolutely nothing. It was so perfectly normal that it almost chills me now. Knowing that they knew." She shook her head, crossing her arms as if to sink in on herself. "I started getting ready for school. Mama was already up, which should have been my first clue that something was off, and then she made eggs, biscuits, and sausage. The only time anyone made breakfast around our house was Daddy on Sunday mornings, and that'd become more rare over the years anyway." She paused, and I took the moment to take her fingers in mine. She smiled up at me before continuing. "And then I went to school. Everything was perfectly fine. The thought actually crossed my mind in my first class that morning that maybe Mama had made breakfast because she felt bad for hitting me the night before." She laughed, uncharacteristic bitterness lacing the sound. "And when I got home from school that day, they were both there, waiting for me. All dressed up next to two small suitcases of what Mama said were the only things I needed for where I was goin' next."

I gnashed my teeth, containing the rage that was pummeling my veins. Thank God her mama and daddy weren't alive now. I couldn't be held responsible for what I might do.

"I fought with them," she whispered, tears sliding down her cheeks. "All I could think about was finding a minute alone to slip out the door and run all the way to your house. I knew if I could just get to you, you wouldn't let them take me."

"Augusta." I crushed her into my chest, heart

thrumming as my own salty tears bled into my beard, soaking the cotton of both of our T-shirts.

I held her closer than I ever had, held her like I'd lost her, because I fucking had. One night she was in my arms, the next vanished.

I'd lost the woman, and somehow, she'd found her way back to me, even after everything we'd both been through.

I murmured the only words I could think of against her ear. "I'm so fucking sorry, Augusta Belle."

SEVENTEEN

Augusta—Ten Years Ago

My head pounded, my eyes blurry as I slowly woke up, cold window pane pressed against my cheek as my parents' car sped down the interstate. "Where are we?"

My dad glanced at me in the rearview mirror, pleased smile on his face. "Oh, the princess is awake."

"Dad, what are we doing? What's wrong?"

"What's wrong?" he crooned, liquid brown eyes locked on mine. "What isn't wrong? You disappear all night, sleeping around with some loser kid, and think as a parent I'm not gonna have something to say about that?"

"That's not what we are—" I defended lamely, eyes searching my father's in the cold mirror, my mother's now turned and addressing me.

"Oh, honey, we just want what's best for you, and I think what we've got planned will be the best thing. We've been thinking a lot about it. Your dad and I have really done our research on this, and believe me when I say—"

"Believe you?" I erupted, haze suddenly clearing a little more from my head. "You drug me to get me into the car, and then tell me I should trust you?"

"I'm sorry you feel that way, Augusta Belle, but if we didn't do everything in our power as your parents to put you on the path to a bright and successful future, well, we just couldn't live with ourselves." My mother's saccharine voice made me cringe.

"That's the problem here, isn't it? You can't live with each other, so you're kicking me out thinking that will solve all your problems?" I assessed the locks in the car, the speed at which my dad was traveling, and debating if I could do some sort of roll that could keep me alive if I launched myself out the door right now. We couldn't be that far from the Choctaw County line, could we?

But I wasn't sure.

It was so fucking dark.

We had to have been in the car for at least three or four hours, which really fucking begged the question about what they'd given me to knock me out for so damn long. And then I remembered my mother's array of prescriptions in her medicine cabinet. If only Fallon were here to see what kind of shit they were pulling now...

Fallon.

My heart was cleaved in half by a ragged edge, tears finally tracking down my face as I thought about how many hours apart we were for the first time in two years. If I'd only known last night was going to be our *last* night.

I swiped angrily at my cheeks, thinking crying would get me no closer to figuring a way out of this car, before my mother turned around again, thrusting a bag of fast food into my lap. "We stopped a few hours ago. It's probably cold, but you were sleeping so peacefully we just didn't want to wake you."

I glared, cold and hard at her. "Why is it that you're being the kindest to me you've ever been in my lifetime when you're driving me god knows where to leave me all by myself?"

For the first time, the mask of kindness fell and her eyes hardened. "This school costs a lot of money. There's no way in or out, and every fucking minute of your day will be structured and logged. Your dad and I can log in and watch you over the cameras."

"Cameras?" I choked, throwing the cold burger and fries to the floor at my feet. "What the fuck is this place? And how long do I have to stay?"

My mother smiled again. She must've taken a

truckload of tranquilizers to manage that smile on her face. "Well, the entire senior year of high school, of course."

"All of it?" I was shrieking again; I couldn't help it. "Can I come home for holidays? Christmas? What about Dad's birthday? We always go out on the lake and—"

"Oh, we have to sell the boat, honey. Your dad is thinking of retiring early. Work has just been so stressful. You know there was some fire at a crack house this morning, and he could hardly get away to drive us down here now. We're so lucky to have him."

I winced, watching as she praised my dad, his eyes glazing over in the mirror as her superficial sweetness seemed to suck him in.

"This is fucking crazy, and I'm not doing it. I'll just run away. I can work."

"We thought about that." My mom turned in the front seat and dug through her purse. "I know that's what most parents would probably do, but that just didn't feel like enough. Our Lady of Sacred Heart sounded like such a nicer option, and look how old it is. I know you like old architecture and things, so when I came across this brochure, I fell in love with it. We had to pay a little extra for the last-minute registration, but they're used to dealing with cases like this. We're lucky they leave a few beds open for sudden problems."

"A bed?" I sobbed, throwing the brochure back into

the front seat. "Why are you doing this? It's just one more year of school. I'll move out, you and Dad can have all the time in the world you want alone again. I'll swim harder than ever this season and make sure I get a scholarship and get into a good school. I promise, Mom, please."

Dad was shaking his head, Mama leaning away from my pleading touch. "No, honey. Not after what your father witnessed…"

"Witnessed? Why does it feel like there's more you're not tellin' me?"

"Well, I guess it just came to our attention recently that you've been dating a boy who's five years older than you."

My eyebrows shot up, surprised that this might have more to do with Fallon than I thought.

"Fallon's good for me. I swear he's been the only thing making me feel sane and stable lately." I couldn't shake the irony tensing all my muscles. I didn't make a practice of hating people, not even those bimbo mean girls at school who were always smoking cigarettes and cussing like that made them cool, but I hated my mother and father in that moment.

I'd resented them for years before now, spent as many nights as I could running away from the toxic chaos they created. And now, after everything, they were taking Fallon from me?

"But what does Fallon do? See, your father's been around his sort for a long time, honey."

"I'm a professional at recognizing a bum, Augusta Belle." He nodded, eyes wide with knowing in the mirror.

I wanted to gouge those cold, dark eyes out of their sockets right now.

"He's not a bum. He saved me."

"Saved you from what?" My mom laughed. "Only thing you needed saving from was him. You know what you did...it's illegal. There's a name for it. It's called statutory rape, Augusta Belle. I told you your father, and I did our research on this."

"But, I... Now? I'm almost an adult. I can make my own fucking decisions!"

"We just want what's best for you, sweetheart. And you may not know it yet, but this school is what's best for you. Like a fresh perspective. Aren't you always sayin' you want out of Choctaw County? Well, now's your chance."

"No, I'm not always saying that." That was a small white lie; I'd been saying that on repeat until the day I turned fifteen. The day Fallon caught me tryin' to jump off the Whiskey River Bridge.

I swallowed the ache in my throat, tired of fighting, knowing they would never see my side of this.

"Well, if I had a nickel for every time I heard you say

you hated that town…" My mom shook her head. "I just can't believe you've been sneakin' out all those nights right under our noses. I mean, it's not like we weren't home. We had family dinner together every night! I just don't understand why you wanted to go out and spend time with a boy like that."

"He's not what you think," I defended quietly, the fight already fading.

"Forgive me if I didn't like the way he had his hands on you, his tongue down your throat first thing in the morning." Dad shook his head, eyes avoiding mine now. "Only time a man touches a woman like that is when he knows her *intimately.*"

I couldn't help the blush that crept up my cheeks. If this were just forty-eight hours before, I would defend our innocent love tooth and nail. But the truth was, on top of all of this, the most beautiful part of the last day was that I'd given my virginity to Fallon.

We'd spent one last wonderful, bittersweet night in each other's arms, crying, kissing, making music, and dreaming of our futures.

"If you woulda told me, Augusta Belle…" My mom fought tears.

"If I woulda told you, you would have dragged me by the hair into the car and robbed me of my life!"

"You're right, I would have. And I also would have gotten one of those doohickeys put in your arm. What do they call it? The birth control so you don't get knocked up by that useless riffraff and ruin your life."

I screwed up my face. "You don't know what you're talking about."

"I looked him up, Augusta Belle. You know anything about his family? They're a rough sort." My dad shook his head, disappointment crossing his features at the thought of his daughter spending time with people like that. "They got generations of crime runnin' through their blood. I looked that boy's daddy up on the system at work and found half a dozen bench warrants, mostly for public intox, but still. What does that man bring to society? You know his daddy's daddy used to own a whiskey still out on the river. Made a lot of money sellin' illegal 'shine back in the day, but not anymore. Now they're all just a bunch of poor, drunk fools, livin' off the rest of us."

"Daddy," I pleaded, thinking more than ever that launching myself out of a moving vehicle sounded like the only appropriate action.

"I mean it, Augusta Belle. Over my dead body will a boy like that lay his hands on you again. Your mama and I raised you better."

I didn't bother responding, defeat now weighing down every single one of my muscles with lead.

I would probably never see Fallon again.

I'd be lucky to even survive this school, much less

make the grades to get into a college without a swimming scholarship. Good grades didn't come easily to me. Swimming did, though. Swimming was my superpower, and now they were sending me to some fucking religious convent off in the swamps of Mississippi, and expected me to be my best self?

I'd have to depend on my parents just to come get me out of the hellhole.

I swallowed the ache in my throat, feeling my tears finally dry for the first time in a while. I sat up a little straighter in the back seat, vowing for the first time in my life that now would be the last time I would see both of their faces.

I didn't need them to succeed; I only needed the strength deep inside myself that I'd been calling on since the first day my parents had begun to lay into each other, regardless of the tender ears hanging on every word upstairs.

They left my home life in a constant state of chaos, nerves on heightened alert as I was always braced to defend myself, fight-or-flight in full effect, twenty-four hours a day with these two.

But not anymore.

They might have stolen my life from me in one sense of the word, but maybe in another, they were giving it back to me.

I would finally be free of them.

I rubbed the spot at my throat where my necklace was missing. The one Fallon had given me.

I nearly lost it then, wishing I had at least that small piece of him to carry with me over the rest of my senior year.

If I was going to make anything of myself, I was damn well determined to do it without the fools sitting in front of me, masquerading as my caring parents.

I could handle the next year of school alone.

I would excel.

And on the day I graduated, I would walk out the doors a fully independent woman, and then head right back to Chickasaw Ridge and track down Fallon Gentry.

We had a life to get started on, and the next few months I was away would just be a small roadblock in our path to happiness. The love Fallon and I had could withstand it. We could withstand anything.

Besides, the only person I knew who was more stubborn than me was Fallon Gentry. He'd move heaven and earth to find out where I was. And when he did, he'd come track me down and steal me away from whatever this god-awful place was they were sending me.

My friends would start calling. Surely, I could write letters. It'd get back to Fallon at some point that I was in Mississippi, and then it would only be a matter of time before he found his way to me.

Little did I know then that the nightmare was just

beginning.

It was what came after that ended up unraveling me, one swift thread at a time.

EIGHTEEN

Fallon

"I cried myself to sleep for months," she whispered, eyes trained on the lines of the freeway blurring out the windshield. "It was unreal. I didn't think I had so many tears."

I couldn't even begin to form words, her story far more fucked-up than I'd thought.

"And then I wrote you a million letters. Three a day for the first few weeks." She shook her head as if she was embarrassed by the silly girl she'd been.

"I wish like hell I'd gotten those letters." My eyes met hers across the cab of my truck. "I woulda come for you. I wouldn't have been able to help myself." I gripped the wheel, so much regret flooding my body. "Your parents were gone for months, out on their boat, I heard later.

Everyone wondered where you went. It was the talk of the town for so fucking long. And then whenever I walked into the corner store, the bar, my goddamn cousin's auto shop, everyone in the room would hush, eyes following my every move as if I knew where you were. As if I'd done something to you." I took a quiet breath. "They looked at me like they wondered if I'd killed you."

She bundled herself up a little tighter in my heavy flannel jacket, sucking in a ragged breath before unbuckling her seat belt and sliding across the bench seat until our thighs were touching.

I breathed a little easier then, havin' her close.

Like the slow burn of warm whiskey down the back of my throat, tingles left on my lips, and surrender in my tired muscles, touching Augusta Belle Branson had been the only crutch I'd needed to get through some of the hardest revelations of my life.

I'd constructed some sort of story in my head about what'd happened the day she left, but it hadn't been anything like what'd really transpired.

I slung my arm around her shoulders, hugging her a little closer to me as we drove on toward Tupelo, leaving our pasts behind and confronting something new every mile along the way.

"Hell, Augusta Belle," I breathed her sweet name from my lips, the sensation it left an intoxicating one. "There was a time I wondered if you were dead." I shook my head, remembering so many sleepless nights, her on my mind. "Those letters woulda been a game changer."

She snuggled into the crook of my arm, one of her little hands resting on the rough denim of my thigh. "I kept them for a long time. Years. I didn't throw them away until I left college. I used to read them on the bad days, but at some point, it was all just too much. I couldn't keep reliving it."

I nodded slowly, for the first time wishing I hadn't been so hard to find. If I woulda parked my ass in Nashville and kept on with the high-profile life, it woulda been easier for her to find me. But that life... I just couldn't keep fakin' it anymore.

"So what was it like there? Your senior year at a school for rich kids who sneak out and kiss kids from the wrong side of the tracks?"

Her grin split her face. "It was an all-girls' school, for starters, with a heavy emphasis on daily routine and discipline. And you weren't there, so that's three strikes."

I laughed, easing the tension inside the cab for the first time in the two hours since we'd left Memphis and hit Highway 22.

Augusta Belle kept working the worn denim of my jeans, a melancholy frown playing across her features.

"Still the saddest girl I've ever known," I breathed into the quiet air.

Her grin tipped up her lips. "Some days lyin' in bed and waitin' for the sadness to pass was all I could do without fallin' apart."

I knew all too goddamn well what she meant.

Except on those days, I'd had whiskey.

It occurred to me again that I thought a fuck of a lot less about whiskey since she'd come around. There was a time my body would shut down into violent shakes I'd been hittin' the bottle so hard, but detoxin' off the hard shit had never come so easy as when I had her to distract me.

Truth was, life in general seemed a helluva lot easier when she was around.

And then I wondered if this was what it would be like to love her.

Let her into my life again.

Let her into my heart.

My palms began to prickle with an unfamiliar ache before I shifted in my seat, eye catching the sign that said we were only five miles outside of Tupelo. I couldn't believe after all these years her first time back in the state was with me, listening to her tell the story of the first time she was here. I liked the idea of being on the road with Augusta Belle, but no way would I ask her to do this with me full time. This was my life.

This road, my truck, the music.

I couldn't walk away from the music; it'd saved me

probably even more than whiskey had.

I would be a selfish fool to think asking her to live like a nomad with me, guitar in hand, would be anything but awful for her. But the plain truth was, the road was the only place that'd been my home for a long time now, long before I'd even met Augusta Belle up top of the Whiskey River Bridge.

I was born with gypsy blood running through my veins. I would never be the type to settle down behind a white picket fence, and all the good things in life were what Augusta Belle was born into. What she deserved.

I never thought the day would come that I could make Augusta Belle deserve me. But she did make me a better man, and that was the most a guy like me could hope for. In fact, if her daddy had had one thing right, it was that she was too good for me. I couldn't give her the things she was used to. At least, not then. Now, was a different ball game.

I'd burned through a lot of my cash living on the road, but I'd also managed to stow a fair bit of it away for rainy days ahead. Bein' a part of Augusta Belle's father's estate wasn't somethin' I'd ever expected, but I didn't need nor want it. That all belonged to Augusta Belle, some small retribution for the hell she'd had to endure in their household, born to be their scapegoat.

If my dad had taught me anything, it was that sometimes a whole life could consist of rainy days. If you got a chance to plan for them, a person ought to.

"Did your parents come down for your graduation?" I asked, as if that were the most important part of this story. But it was, somehow.

She shook her head, sweet lips turning down as it looked like she might dissolve into tears. "Nah, they skipped it."

I nodded, no words I could give her to soothe that kind of pain.

"It was better that way," she offered bravely with a shrug. "I probably would have been so nervous seeing them for the first time. At least I was able to focus. Graduated top of the *very* small class that year, and it earned me a few extra scholarships." She pulled on the bottom of her lip, eyes focused out the windshield at the horizon. "Didn't see Mama again until…" She swallowed. "Well, the first time I went back home was after she was diagnosed."

Old wounds bled between us in the cab, but for the first time, they weren't ours.

"Sometimes I wish I would have had more moments with her, maybe we could have had the conversations we needed to. But I have to say, Fallon…" She pressed her lips together, holding back tears. "She never really seemed like…she never had that mom moment for me, y'know?" Her eyes met mine, seeking understanding.

"I know." I understood perfectly. I'd had the same sort

of experience with my own parents. My mom, to this day, still in and out of rehab, struggling with her own demons. And my dad so racked with pain and bitterness the duration of his life he could never see outside of it long enough to spend a real moment with his kids, much less hold a job. Even in the end, he only asked for help, never a single moment between us beyond what I could do for him physically.

I swallowed down that old familiar burn.

"Did you ever talk to them about…" I struggled to find the right words. "That night?"

"Not really." She sighed. "It all happened so fast. I did what I could to help her, and then after… Well, after, Dad just wasn't the same. It was weird. The last time I was in that house, it was so much chaos, so much fighting. Fast-forward a few years and all of a sudden everything's changed. Dad had to adjust to Mom being gone, and I had to adjust to the man I thought I knew."

I nodded, thinking it was probably pretty similar to what she'd had to do with me.

"It wasn't much long after Mama was gone that I noticed he was starting to slip. I couldn't put my finger on it at first. Just one day, it was one thing. A month later, a few more. So I came home to help him over the winter. Really, I think just the thought of him alone in that big old house…" Soft tears wet her eyelashes. "I wasn't even home a year, and we found out his immune system was compromised. His lungs weren't in good shape from smoking all the Dunhills, and the vodka, well…"

I remembered the faint smell of cloved smoke that usually lingered around her front porch where her dad often sat, puffing in the corner with a glass of his favorite Russian formula.

It was weird, spendin' so much time with a family without them even realizin' I was there. In a lot of ways, I was a ghost to the Bransons, someone who haunted the periphery, never quite important enough to make it all the way into their world.

It'd struck me a lot of nights how lucky I was that Augusta Belle wasn't anything like either of her parents. She was kind and sweet, full of compassion and a supercharged sense of adventure. A smile still turned up my lips when I thought of the countless nights of fun we'd had, just her and me, my guitar and the moonlight.

If Augusta Belle had been anything like her parents, she probably would have looked through me that first day up on the bridge. I wouldn't have been a blip on her radar.

I couldn't imagine the endless dark days and nights I would have had without her sunshine.

A man couldn't live without the sunshine. I knew; I'd been doin' it day in and day out for too many years now. "Wish I woulda been around to help you then."

Her face was soft, reflective. "I'm glad I had that time

with him. Spent my whole life resenting the life they'd brought me into, and then all of a sudden…" She shrugged, finally catching my eyes. "Life."

"Ain't that the truth." I slid my palm over her knee, giving it a soft squeeze along with a smile.

"Stayed up late so many nights, lyin' on the roof outside of my room and watchin' the stars. Writing music and wondering if we were both watchin' the same moon turn into the same dawn light every mornin'." She smiled up at me, the first genuine slice of happiness I'd seen on her face since we'd left Memphis. "Made me feel grounded, looking up at how big the universe is and knowin' you could see it too. It was the only connection I had."

I swallowed, the vulnerable side of her something I wasn't used to. "We're only a few miles from the hotel. I know it's late, but I thought we could get something a little nicer tonight. Been so used to being by myself, I didn't really think about what that last place might have been like from a lady's perspective."

"A lady's perspective?" She giggled, tucking her arm under my elbow and smiling. "Since when have you ever treated me like a lady, Gentry?"

I grinned, shaking my head when I thought of all the times I'd held the door, held her hand, helped her out of the car, sang her to sleep… "You may be a lady now, Augusta Belle, but you'll always be my whiskey girl."

She paused, smile faltering for an instant before she recovered. "It's weird, knowin' I'm…*her.*"

I thought about the woman I sang of who'd left my heart sliced open on the floor. A rousing third chorus line I'd added to a lot of bootleg performances in the earlier days. I winced, wondering if she'd heard any of those versions.

"You're not, not really. That was my perception of things at the time, but I'm not that kid anymore either." I tapped my fingertips on the wheel as I mused out loud. "The person I am on the stage, the one they think they're getting, the one they paid money for, I have to give them at least some of that even if that's not entirely the man I am. Working in the public eye, it's a weird thing."

She yawned, leaning her head on my shoulder.

"Rest your eyes. I'll wake you up when we get there. And if you're lucky, maybe I'll even carry you upstairs so you don't have to use your legs."

She laughed. "That sounds so ladylike."

"Doin' the best I can here, baby." I gave her my best sideways Elvis impersonation. "Welcome to Tupelo."

"Think you're cute?" We both erupted into a laugh when the "Welcome to Tupelo" and "Elvis Presley Birthplace" signs were illuminated by my headlights a moment later.

Augusta Belle made everything about being on the

road better; there was no doubt about that.

I wasn't sure what in the hell the future held for us—not a damn thing was most likely—but right then, I made a point not to give a shit and live in every moment, enjoyin' the sunshine and smiles of Augusta Belle Branson while I had 'em.

NINETEEN

Fallon

By the time we'd checked in to our hotel, which for a midnight staff took longer than it damn well should have, Augusta was wide awake, singing full songs under her breath and interjecting her own, often more clever lyrics into the stanzas.

Just as the clock was inching past three in the morning, she was breaking into a rendition of Queen I'd never quite heard before. "This performance has been truly awe-inspiring, but a few hours of sleep would probably be the adult thing."

"Let's go for a walk." She dug through her backpack and found something long-sleeved to pull over herself, and she was opening the door, eyes on me and waiting.

"You're shittin' me."

She shook her head, grin widening by each aggravating second.

I shoved a hand through my hair, not even considering for more than a half a second tellin' her no.

I grinned, pullin' my own jacket back over my shoulders and followin' her out the door.

After dropping into an all-night convenience store for hot coffee and a bag of the freshest donuts I'd ever sunk my teeth into, we crossed the river and ambled through neighborhoods and rows of old homes.

She told me about the girls she'd gone to school with in Mississippi, how she kept in touch with none of them because the reminder of why they were all there was just too much. She filled me in on her favorite professors in college, and how she'd never spent so many sleepless nights as she did in the hours leading up to her biology exams.

And she kept writing.

Music felt like the one thing pullin' us together. Was it the thing that would eventually pull us apart?

We watched the dawn come up over the horizon, church steeples as far as the eye could see, our bottoms planted firmly on the little front porch of the tiny white clapboard home Elvis was born in. She'd thought it was ridiculous that the museum didn't open until nine, and when I pointed out that was pretty par for the course with museums, she stated defiantly that *I* was ridiculous.

Augusta Belle, tellin' me the sky was green just to argue.

Augusta'd peeked into all the windows, hands up to the glass and nose pressed to the pane like a little kid, and hell if experiencin' it all with her hadn't made my heart skip a beat.

Being with her again felt like seein' the world through new eyes, and damn if that didn't feel good after living gig to gig all alone on the road.

Maybe that old man was right. Maybe I had seen too much, but who the hell hadn't?

And what could we do about it?

Not a goddamn thing. My own crime had been spendin' so much time dwellin' on what I'd thought happened.

"It's amazing all the things this guy did so young." She referred to Elvis with a swipe of her hand, gesturing to the house behind us. "Some people are just born to break every mold."

"My mama was always singin' along to old Elvis songs when I was a kid—before she got hooked on things she couldn't get away from. We're only as strong as our weakest vice, I guess. This man made all that music in only twenty years. Changed the game the way he brought blues and bluegrass sounds together and created rock 'n' roll. Imagine all the ways he could have kept revolutionizing if…" I trailed off, mind runnin' wild as I thought about my own experience in Nashville. "If the machine wouldn't have eaten him up."

Augusta Belle edged herself a little closer, her soft scent invading my nostrils. "You excited for the show tonight?"

I was pulled from my thoughts, rubbing a hand through my beard. "Don't really get excited anymore."

"Really?" she asked. "Isn't that a problem, then?"

"A problem?" I laughed. "Not that I know of."

"I mean…" She uncrossed her legs, recrossing the opposite way as the shadows turned to light around us. "Aren't you supposed to like your job?"

"I do." I shrugged.

"Well, do you ever want to do something in music that excites you again?"

"Meaning what?" I rubbed at the back of my neck, the three hours in the truck finally catchin' up to my old bones.

"I dunno. I guess I just mean you're better than sticky dive bars and watered-down whiskey." Her eyes focused on a point off in the distance.

"Those sticky dive bars are my home," I replied.

"Sure, but maybe there's something else."

"Nah, there's not."

She shook her head, exasperation creeping into her voice. "One bad experience in Nashville doesn't mean the whole industry is bad."

"If you'd been there, you'd realize that, yes. Yes, it is."

She continued on. "Carve your own way in this business, that's all I'm saying. You have way more talent than even you know, Fallon Gentry. Whatever happens, don't ever doubt that."

I turned her words over in my mind, wondering if she was right. I loved being onstage, but maybe that time of my life was over. I suddenly didn't feel the burning desire to chase something off in the distance—or to run from a past that wouldn't stay there.

"First light of day is always my favorite," she mused, arms pressed into the worn wood of the old but recently painted porch we were probably illegally trespassing on at that moment.

"Somethin' about mornin', starting over, sunshine on your face, can't be beat." A beam of sunlight peeked over the steeple of the church across the street, splitting the light into two fractals and creating a halo.

"It's beautiful," she said, voice sounding far off. "It's the most peaceful moment of the day. I never knew what the next minute might bring when I was growing up in such a chaotic situation, but in that split second, I always knew I was okay."

I looped one of my fingers with hers, giving her a quick nod before lookin' up to the sun and wishin', not for the first time in my life, that Augusta Belle and I could just be left alone. We didn't need any more shit the universe had to throw us because we were really fucking good right here, just like this.

"Come on, Augusta Belle. Nothin' good came of the last time I kept you out till dawn."

She shook her head, threading her fingers between mine before, hand in hand, we stood and walked down the little tree-lined path that led up to Elvis's house, no looking back for either one of us from that point forward.

And for the first time, I thought maybe music was the blessing that knit her and me together, not just the glue we relied on.

No woman had ever understood me the way this one did. It was true then and even truer now.

TWENTY

Fallon

After two nights singin' at Rooster's Blues of Tupelo, Augusta and I hit the road south, a giant fold-out map of the state of Mississippi in her lap and braids in her hair. Her scuffed-up short leather boots told me she'd probably been kickin' around in them since the time I'd known her last. And the way she smiled, coffee in a to-go cup in her hand, did something wild and crazy to my heart.

Made it flip like a schoolgirl despite every badass bone in my body.

Kept those sentiments to myself, though, because bein' worthy of Augusta meant doin' what was right, not sayin' all the pretty things to make her love me again.

Truth was, I didn't want her love if she couldn't love

the man I was now. I didn't even know if I was lookin' for it, but it sure felt good wakin' up to her every morning. Hummin' her to sleep at night was just about perfect too. I had a hard time thinkin' of anything wrong between Augusta Belle and me until I started thinkin' about our past. But truth be told, it'd been startin' to feel like maybe that was something we could get over too.

"Grabbed this for you at the last store we stopped at." I pulled a keychain out of my pocket, Elvis in glittery bold letters on one side, Tupelo, MS emblazoned on the other.

"This is great!" She grabbed it from my fingers, turning it over as her fingernails traced the letters. "We'll always have Tupelo."

"And Elvis," I added seriously.

"So…how much of an off-the-beaten-path kinda guy are ya these days?"

Hesitation was runnin' through my blood at just her words. "Got somethin' on your mind?"

Her thousand-watt smile hit me across the distance between us, and I wanted nothin' more than to press my lips to hers, pull this fucking truck over, throw away everythin' that'd been comin' between us, and make the world right again.

The idea that I'd only tasted her once, only felt her under my palms one night for a few all-too-brief hours had my chest aching in a way I didn't even care to explain.

"See, there's this state park just off the highway." She pointed to a shade of evergreen on the map.

"And you want to go for a nature hike?" I screwed up my face, tryin' to make sense of her request.

"The brochure in the hotel last night showed a massive swimmin' hole." Her grin grew. "With cliff-jumpin'."

"Oh Christ."

"I knew that'd be your first response, but hear me out. The sun on your face, the cool spring water rinsin' every care in the world away…"

"I don't have much for cares lately, but 'preciate your concern about it."

She screwed her eyes shut, pushing a hand over her face and then sighing. "Just thought it would be fun, for old times' sake."

"Old times?" I growled. "Got no need to revisit old times. I'm really fucking good at the moment."

"Well…maybe I just want to go for a swim," she ventured finally.

"Now, that's a request I can accommodate. Which exit am I headed to?"

Her cheeks lit with a radiant smile before she threw herself across the truck, sneaking a kiss at my neck.

I stifled a slow groan, long-dead arousal finally awakening.

"It's the next exit." I would have laughed, but Augusta Belle was sliding her hand through my beard, resting her fingertips along my jawline and brushing her lips across my cheekbone.

Hell, something about her touch lit a fire in my bones.

Swear I would die a happy man as long as I was in this woman's arms.

Where I wouldn't like to die at all was saving this woman as she swan-dived off a cliff face.

Something about Augusta Belle and adrenaline went hand in hand.

"Looks pretty fucking high from this vantage point," I found myself mumbling a few miles later.

We were still driving up the dusty trail that led to the parking area when she squealed, pointing out my window as we both watched a brave swimmer launch themselves over the cliff.

I shuddered when he smacked the water.

"You're insane."

"Just keep driving. It looks amazing."

"You're the stubbornest woman I've ever known."

"Thought I was the saddest?" She shot me a wild, heart-stopping grin.

"I'm revising my opinion."

"Convenient." She arched an eyebrow in challenge, and just as I was about to pull her across the seat and dive lips-first into her, she was pushing open the door and waving me on with her.

I shook my head, following her out of the parking lot and down the dirt path that led to the edge of the cliff.

She pulled her T-shirt over her head, triangles of a small black bikini peeking out at me.

She'd filled out a helluva lot since the last time I'd seen her in a bathing suit, and I liked it. Her soft curves begged for my fingertips, my teeth, all the love I had to spoil her with.

She pushed down her jeans, one leg at a time, before tossing them at me. "Hold my pants?"

I couldn't help the laugh, eyes crinkling up before she blew me a kiss and spun, walking on confident steps to the edge of the cliff. She smiled at the few kids lingering around the edge, hanging out and watching as she hovered, taking in the water, imagining the drop, before she turned, throwing me a wink and then taking a few steps back before sprinting toward the edge. My heart suspended in midair, and my breath caught in my throat when she went over.

I'd seen her do this a hundred times over the years, but nothing ever prepared me for the moment she went over, free-falling into the abyss without any safety net to catch her.

I didn't like it, but I was proud as hell of her every time she did it.

I wasn't man enough to confront my fears as head on

as she did.

"She's cool as shit," one of the kids mused, nodding at me.

I nodded. "Even cooler, man. I can't keep up."

He took me in with his eyes, my worn dark jeans with holes, tattered to the threads. Tattoos swallowing my hands and boots not meant for the Southern sun. But it didn't seem to matter to him, and Augusta Belle certainly didn't give a fuck about the way I looked.

Or at least, she'd never expressed a concern about it before. But walkin' into any hotel we'd been to the last few days, anyone in their right mind probably thought I'd stolen her from the hand of God himself.

She was all sweet and soft and innocent porcelain features, the light to my dark all day long, and yet she was stronger than I could ever hope to be.

I waved at the kids, taking off down the trail that led to the water's edge to find my girl and congratulate her on one stellar jump.

I met her at the shore just as she was climbing out, cold water dripping off her body, a gigantic smile spreading her round cheeks.

"That was incredible. You should try it."

I wrapped my jacket around her shoulders, as concerned she'd catch a cold as much as I was of someone seeing her in a suit so damn small. "I'm super-good with living, thanks."

She shook her head, pressing up on her toes and planting a kiss on my lips. "Thanks for bringing me."

"Your lips on mine is all the thanks I need."

Her cheeks turned a warm shade of crimson before I led her into the sunlight, the flat face of a giant boulder the perfect place for us to spread out. I stripped out of my shirt, laying it down on the rock before settling us both back onto it, my arms cradling her from the rough edges.

"So did you go to school for swimming?"

She looked up, surprise etched on her face. "No. No pool at the school I was at, so it wasn't even an option."

I thought of her parents and all they'd taken away from her that night.

And then I thought of all they may have given her.

I didn't think I was in a place to give her anything—I hardly was now, but there was no doubt I wasn't then.

My mind trailed back to all the nights after the fire I'd had to help my dad in and out of bed, feed him his medication, and help him with therapy. My sister and I had taken on the job full time, and it'd nearly sunk both of us.

No way could I have been there for her in those moments.

"You know the song about the old willow?" she whispered, voice warm with sun and memories.

"Yeah." I traced circles along her bare shoulder,

fingertips dipping in and out of the little black bikini strap that held the triangles in place.

"What made you write that one?"

I heaved a breath, remembering the night in Nashville I'd drained a bottle of cheap rye and wrote my heart out, furious tears in my eyes as the music torched every raw nerve. "That one's about my dad, actually."

She stayed silent for long beats, one china-white calf contrasted against the dark of my jeans as she pondered what to say next. "I really like that one."

I nodded, waiting long moments before adding, "He never went to church, so the pastor wouldn't give him a proper service, but he did offer to speak if I found a burial site. Turns out a person should be a part of a community to be buried in one." I shrugged. "No one wants a drifter."

The words hung thick between us.

"So I found the only place in all of Tennessee I decided I wouldn't mind seein' again. Under that old willow at the back of the field we used to go to."

Tears welled up in her troubled eyes before she spoke. "I'm sorry I wasn't there. I think that's the greatest regret I have."

"Ah, Augusta Belle, life's too short to fuss about regrets." I swallowed my own ball of regret fighting to consume me.

"S'pose we should get back on the road," I breathed,

eyes shuttering closed under the warm sunlight.

"Want me to drive for a while?" she offered, clasping our fingers together and doing her best to pull me off the rock.

I gave in, stretching as I stood up, her small little arms locking around my waist and holding me in a tight hug.

My measured breaths seemed to soothe her as our chests moved in sync, my hands working into the long, wet locks of her hair as my chin hovered just above the crown of her head. "Honey and peaches, damn I missed that smell."

Her arms locked a little tighter around my waist, fingertips digging into the flesh under my T-shirt as soft sobs began a slow shake of her shoulders.

"You okay?" I whispered at her ear, feeling a torrent of shivers race through her body when my body drifted so close to hers.

"Better than okay." She sniffed once, and I wiped at a tear lingering on her cheek. "Just wish we wouldn't have lost so much time."

"Ah." I smiled. "There you go with regrets again." I unpretzled our bodies, threading our fingers, and heading back the way we'd come. "Best thing I learned over the last decade was livin' in the moment is the only life worth livin'." We reached my truck, and I helped her into the passenger side, giving her a peck on the lips when I could steal it. "I'm all about takin' this, whatever this is between us, one day at a time. That all right with you, sunshine?"

Her grin split open before she tugged at the collar of my shirt, pulling me in and locking her ankles around my waist. "That sounds fantastic."

I pushed my lips against hers, splitting the seam as our tongues worked together, hands spreading across bare skin as we ate up the sunshine pulsing between us. I slid my hands around her waist, hiking her farther up the front seat and following up after her, pulling the door closed behind me, locking my lips with hers again.

Her fingertips worked across my neck, slipping under my shirt and sending pulses of raw need throbbing between my legs.

"We need to get to Jackson." I could hear the barely veiled restraint in my own voice.

"Let's just camp out here." Her tone lowered an octave, sweeter than honey.

"Christ, Augusta Belle." I worked my hips between her damp thighs, grinding down on my back teeth as I thought about puppies and Grandma's fried liver and any other damn thing I could manage, to keep myself reined in at this moment.

It'd been so fucking long.

All I could think about was what would happen if I hurt her.

"Don't stop," she whispered at my neck, her lips

touching my skin.

"Fuck," I breathed, everything inside of me wantin' inside of her at that moment.

"Please." She arched her hips, her hand drawing mine up to knead at the heavy flesh of her breast.

"Everything in me is sayin' take you right now, Augusta Belle," I murmured at her earlobe. "But trust me when I say you don't know what you're asking for."

She pushed her nails into my skin, making me wince as she wiggled around underneath me, driving me a little more insane with every damn movement. "I'm ready."

I laughed. "You act brave, sweet bird." My nose danced across the angle of her jawline, her nipples sharpening beneath the triangles of her swimsuit. "Care to tell me why your heartbeat is flickering faster than a hummingbird's wings at your throat?"

Perfect white teeth sank into the aroused flesh of her lips as the tiniest of moans breezed past.

I slammed my eyes closed, needing to erase the face she made when she was so turned on she was about to combust under my hands. "Sing louder, pretty bird."

She swallowed, gaze flickering on mine when I dragged my aroused length along her seam. Soft shudders coursed through every muscle in her body before she clamped down on my shoulder, hips rocking in a silent rhythm to mine before I ducked my head, clasping my lips at the soft outline of one pert nipple and sucking.

Low, serrated gasps fell from her lips before she was moaning once, twice, a third time louder until I angled myself a little deeper, sucking her sweet, damp flesh into my mouth a little harder. She was shuddering and moaning and heaving desperate pants of air against my chest.

"Fuck, you're the most beautiful thing I've ever seen."

Tiny little tears formed at the corners of her eyes before she loosened her fingertips on my shoulders and came back down to earth, eyes finally focusing on mine.

I didn't know what she was thinking in that moment. I couldn't even put a finger on exactly what I was thinkin', but I felt it.

Whatever was passing between us was supercharged. Somethin' words could only cheapen.

She was silky and sensual, smoky on the lips, warm on the tongue, smooth on the way down.

She was whiskey.

And I was hooked.

TWENTY-ONE

Fallon

"That was the longest ride of my life, almost literally."
She flopped onto the bed, backpack flying beside her.

"Almost literally?" I tossed my wallet and keys onto the
nearest surface and fell into the massive king with her.

A king room was the last they had, but she'd taken to
sleepin' at my side all night anyway, so the extra bed we'd
had before now was always a waste. It was odd, how
quickly I started adjusting to her presence,
accommodating her needs, thinking of her before myself.

Wasn't used to that at all, but being with Augusta Belle
was just so easy.

She held up her phone, punching in the password for
the Wi-Fi before opening one of her many social media
apps. I watched her scroll mindlessly before a notification

182

popped up that she had 99+ new friend requests.

"What the hell?" She frowned. "I don't recognize any of these people."

She gnawed on her bottom lip, and hell if I didn't want to be the one gnawing on it right now. I flipped onto my side, running a hand up her ankle, sliding my fingers to the tender spot under her knees before creeping up her inner thigh.

"Holy shit, Fallon."

I grinned, adding a second hand to her other thigh, ready as fuck to continue the path we'd been on earlier.

"Fallon, look." She turned her screen around, thrusting it in my face.

"I can't read that shit. Gives me a headache." I ducked, nipping at the outside of her knee, dragging a tongue across the elegant indent that always made her squirm.

"Fallon, I don't think you're getting this right now, but we're front page on TMZ."

My hands fell, eyes slamming closed as I fell back into a world I'd escaped not long enough ago.

"What the fuck?" I pulled the phone from her outstretched hand, scrolling the bullshit text of what they claimed was a breaking story, that ex-country rocker Fallon Gentry had found his whiskey girl again.

I winced.

"They have my name, Fallon."

I attempted swallowing the lump clogging my throat. "Saw that."

"What if they start digging into my past, what if they find out about my parents and us and just…*everything?*"

"They will," I muttered, pushing myself off the bed, eyes on the minibar instantly.

My fingers twitched, a slow ache settling at the base of my skull that I couldn't shake.

Jim Beam. Jack Daniel's. Maybe a local oak-aged. I wondered what a place like this would offer in the minibar. Probably just vodka. I'd have to hit the nearest liquor store if that was the case.

I groaned, realizing that old train of thought was eating up my insides again.

I hadn't had a drop of whiskey since Augusta Belle'd walked back into my life.

Well, almost. There had been that bender, but hell if I could do that again.

I heaved a breath, tortured by what to even offer next. "They have your name, so we're pretty much fucked." I pushed a hand through my hair and stalked across the room. "Shoulda expected this. It's my fault. I shouldn't have let you up onstage that first night in Memphis. It was too much publicity. Hell, give 'em another day, and they'll be down here with boom microphones in our faces."

Augusta Belle's eyes watered as she sat cross-legged on

the bed, eyes fixed on the screen in her hands, fingers already trembling. "I can't let that happen."

"It already is, sunshine." The endearment I'd called her earlier didn't have quite the same ring as it had hours ago.

"No, Fallon." Her irises widened, and she pressed up on her knees until she was eye level with me, inching closer until her hands were within reach. "That can't happen."

"I know it's gonna suck, believe me, been there. But we'll get through it. Maybe get you a wig or something. And no more singing onstage, all that…*sexual chemistry* just attracts them like honeybees." I held her wrists, preparing to pepper them with reassuring kisses when she yanked them away and leaped off the bed.

She shook her head back and forth, eyes sliding everywhere around the room but on me. "What if they find out about—" She pulled out her backpack, tearing out some papers she had and perusing them quickly. "I wonder if there's any other documentation…"

"Oh, if there's documentation, they'll find it." I hovered over her shoulder, planting a hand on the dip of her spine in the hopes of calming her.

"No, Fallon, no! You don't understand." She finally looked up, her eyes wet with tears and terror that stole all the breath from my fucking lungs.

"What, Augusta Belle? What's wrong?" I slid a hand

into her hair, my palm at the back of her soft neck.

"There's more." She swallowed. "There's one more thing I haven't told you about."

I nodded, unable to form a word, trying to blink some sort of silent signal to encourage her on, but the truth was, I didn't think I wanted her to.

I wasn't sure I was ready for whatever else she was about to tell me.

"I spent so many nights crying, so many nights wondering what I could have done different. I could hardly eat. Missing you was the darkest time of my life, Fallon." She wrung her hands, swallowing again before her eyes darted from my gaze to my lips and back again. "I missed you so much those first few weeks at school…" Fresh tears tracked down her cheeks. "I didn't even know I was pregnant."

TWENTY-TWO

Augusta—Nine Years Ago

Tears of pain cut quietly down my cheeks as I winced, trying not to squirm as the doctor pressed apart my thighs, encouraging me to relax.

"This will only take a minute, sweetheart."

I cringed at his term of endearment, wishing the nurse was at least still in here with me, someone to make me feel not so alone on this cold hospital bed, feet in stirrups.

"Have you seen the baby move yet?" He grinned, popping out from behind the sheet covering my lower half.

I swallowed razors and squeaked, "No."

"Should be any time, most women see an elbow or a foot pop out over the last few weeks."

I swallowed again, fear spinning through my stomach as I wished like hell he was here with me.

Fallon.

After each girl was enrolled at Sacred Heart for four weeks, a customary blood test was taken.

A test that checked for a lot of things: diseases, disorders, pregnancy.

And that's when I'd found out.

Not wrapped in Fallon's arms, our eyes shedding happy tears as we planned our lives together.

But 500 miles away in the middle of nowhere, all alone.

There were other girls who were pregnant. Apparently, it wasn't uncommon, considering many of the girls who showed up at Sacred Heart came from a sketchy past. This was usually their last resort before juvenile detention.

Once the administrators found out I was pregnant, they moved me to another wing. I shared a room with three other girls who were each expecting, little privacy for homework or reading or crying.

I was still writing Fallon letters.

I couldn't stop.

I knew I'd never send them, but they weren't for him anyway. They were for me.

"There ya are, sweetheart." The doctor patted my knee, my legs falling closed.

I clamped down on my lip, feeling violated not for the first time since I'd been coming to these "prenatal appointments" in the basement of the school. The building wasn't set up to house a hospital wing, they said, so they'd done very little to spruce up the place and forced us to see a local doctor once a month, outdated equipment tagging along with him.

I'd written my parents early on, begged them to come and get me, told them we could raise the baby together. The house was big enough, I could get my GED, I conjured every happy ending in my head before I realized there wasn't one coming.

There were no such thing as happy endings, and if I was going to survive, I'd have to save myself.

I wandered back to my room, cold tile floor under my feet as the opening line of "Whiskey Girl" started playing in my mind.

It's not easy to forget, the bitter taste lovin' you left...

That same damn song was running through my head another day.

Not a week later, walking into advanced calculus, my water broke, soaking my sneakers and the floor all around them.

Real tears welled up in my eyes as one girl had sneered, whispered about the no-good rich whore having her baby.

The nurses were promising me minutes later that I

would soon be holding my baby, that they would let me feed our child, body naked and warm and small against my own. Tiny fingers and toes, steady heartbeat, and his first breathfuls of air as he came screaming into the world. The nurses promised me all of it.

And I hung my future on those hopes.

Once the nurses changed me into a birthing gown and settled me into bed, an IV of fluids puncturing my vein, my limbs were suddenly heavy, eyelids slowly fading before the world was gone a few minutes later.

My next moments of consciousness punctuated by a sense of hope.

My heart felt lighter, as if holding our baby in my arms, knowing I only had a month before I graduated and we could finally start the life we'd been planning, was just around the corner. I was so foolish believing in that dream, assuming we could start again right where we'd left off.

It was the feeling of hope that haunted me after my life was stolen from me a second time.

I called for the nurses, surprised when I found myself in my dorm room, all alone in the middle of the day.

I felt tender, I felt raw, and little did I know I'd just given birth to a tiny human destined to be a stranger.

The nurses bustled in then, smiles on their faces as they tended to my bandages.

Pretending like nothing had happened.

"Where's my baby?" The words croaked out of my throat.

"Oh, honey. You just need to focus on your classes now."

I swallowed, disbelieving of her words. "Where's my baby?"

She smiled with her eyes, lips held tight as she patted my knee. "I'll go get your breakfast, dear, and then maybe you want to work on your calculus? Success favors those who work hard, Augusta."

She closed the door, leaving me all alone, my thoughts buzzing at a million miles a second. "My baby," I whispered, wincing, crawling out of bed, and feeling a searing pain in my abdominal muscles. "Where's my baby?"

Violent tears streamed down my cheeks, the horror of my reality slowly settling into all the dark nooks and crannies.

"My baby!" I screamed again, making my way to the window, decorative wrought-iron bars meant to disguise their real purpose—to cage me in. "Bring me my baby."

I crumpled into a heap, laying my cheek on the worn wooden plank floor and sobbing until my entire body ached, the pain in my abdomen long forgotten because the pain of losing a piece of my soul ravaged more.

"Someone stole my baby," I mumbled, not even registering when the door creaked open a while later, soft hands pulling me up by the elbows. A tenderer touch than I'd had since the night I left Fallon's arms.

Fallon.

I ached the deepest for Fallon.

He'd probably long forgotten me, his life as a big-city music star an existence far beyond my wildest imagination.

"I missed the first breaths. I missed holding…" My heart cracked in two jagged pieces, shredding my insides as they landed on the floor at my feet. "I don't even know if…if I had a boy or a girl." My face crumpled, devastated tears swallowing me whole. "I was going to go home. We were gonna raise the baby together."

"You'll get over it, dear. One day you'll learn, there really isn't ever any going home." The headmistress, a woman I'd spoken to once on the day my parents had dropped me off here and only seen lurking the hallways silently since then, was now tucking the white sheets around my shoulders, nodding once over her shoulder before the nurse from earlier stepped up. "This will be better for you, dear. The less you remember, the better it is, we've found."

I opened my mouth to protest before soft straps were looped around my wrists and anchored to a hospital bed.

I tried to overpower them, but the screaming pain in my abdomen, the reminder of everything I'd lost in a single blink, halted any drive I had to fight. Frustrated tears leaked out of my eyes, the need to stay strong and silent more powerful than ever.

"My baby…"

I locked eyes with the headmistress, hovering above my face as the nurse pushed a tiny needle into the vein at my elbow, my muscles relaxing almost instantly before my eyelids grew heavy and I was gone.

The second time in my life I'd lost my everything.

TWENTY-THREE

Fallon

"I graduated a month later, still healing from the child they'd ripped from my body. I smiled, pretending like they hadn't stolen the only thing precious to me." Her eyes darted up, flooded with hopeless tears. "I never knew if he had your silky brown eyes or if she had a dusting of my freckles on the top of her nose."

An ache, deep and dark, burrowed its way into my guts, bitterness rising up in my throat over all that'd happened without me. "I don't even know what to say."

She hesitated at my shoulder, eyes glued to mine as if waiting for my response.

I didn't have one.

I was fucking dumbstruck.

I'd had a lot of punches thrown my way in life, but

this one, I'd never seen coming.

"To be honest, Augusta Belle…" My tone was laced with more anger than I'd intended. "I'm having an issue understanding why you didn't say anything before now."

"Before now? You mean like, last week? When was I supposed to tell you?"

"I dunno. Woulda expected the mother of my child to track me the fuck down at her earliest convenience, of course." The sneer hit its mark, her face twisting with a wince.

"You disappeared! Never came back to Chickasaw. How did I know where to find you?"

"Fucking really, Augusta? At that time, everyone knew where to find me. I had TMZ up my ass every goddamn day!"

She locked her lips, eyes flaring with unspeakable anger, a grown-up side to Augusta I hadn't quite witnessed before that moment.

"If you wanted to find me, you would've." I yanked open the door on the minibar, swiping every tiny bottle of whiskey I could find, uncapping the first and throwing back the numbing shot.

I uncapped the next and did the same, before dumping both empties in the garbage can. I opened the third and final, tossing the top in the garbage and readying to swallow the remainder. "You had my fucking baby"—searing tears stung my eyelids—"and you hid it from me."

"It wasn't like that. I was just waiting for the right time."

"The right time?" I roared, finishing the last bottle of booze and hurling it across the room. It shattered into a thousand tiny shards against the window. Augusta's own tears were fresh and flowing faster as she ran into the bathroom, slamming the door closed and locking it.

I stood in the silence, hearing her soft sobs on the other side of the door, wondering what the fuck I'd done to deserve all of this.

When Augusta brought the sunshine, it inevitably caused a burn.

My mouth watered as the tingly sensation in my body grew, whiskey workin' its way through my tired bones.

I suddenly felt every single one of my thirty-three years like a ton of baggage weighing down my shoulders.

With the sound of her tears in the back of my head, I walked on long strides out of the door, down the hallway, and angled for the liquor store down the block I'd spotted on the way in.

I might have been a reformed alcoholic for the last few days, but that shit changed now.

Anticipation rocketed through my veins as I neared the neon, open-all-night signs, steps quickening as the sound of old, moody classic rock songs filtered into my ears.

A dive bar.

Home.

I ventured through the ancient front door, the live music loud as fuck, bass line pumping through my heart like a lullaby. I reached the bar, tapped twice on the sticky varnished wood and ordered two doubles, throwing a fifty in the tip jar as I told them to keep them comin'.

Seven drinks later, I made a decision to stop counting, my muscles finally losing the tension as a new band came onstage, a four-piece set that cranked the bass even louder, everyone in the bar crossing toward the dance floor as they sang about tequila nights.

"They're good!" a voice called through the chaos, sidling up to my shoulder and making a shiver run down my spine.

Peaches, but spicier. Cinnamon, maybe.

"They're not bad." I swallowed the rest of my drink, eyes blurring just a little as I tried to focus on the woman standing at my side.

"You an expert or somethin'?" Her deep drawl was foreign to my ears. The only woman I'd been attuned to had a softer lilt to her twang. Like a bird. My bird.

I tapped the bar, two more doubles required to wash away that memory.

"I'm somethin'," I finally muttered.

"You got a chip on your shoulder, is that what it is?"

"Wouldn't be in here if I didn't, s'pose."

She, whoever she was, scrunched up her eyes, edging a little closer with her gaze lingering on my lips. "I might be able to help with that."

I shook my head, taking another shot and clearing the glass. This time, the burn not quite so satisfying as it had been. "Got somethin' smoother? Top-shelf?"

The bartender shrugged. "That's as top-shelf as it gets 'round here, buddy."

I swallowed another gulp, no longer giving a fuck what it tasted like.

Everything hurt right now.

From the inside out, she'd mutilated me.

That was probably why, an hour later, I found myself tucked into a corner booth behind the stage, a new band screaming about hot Southern dreams as the pounding in my head grew to a deafening blast.

Alyvia with an A, *and a Y,* as she'd earlier announced, was wiggling in my lap, her hands in a lot of places they shouldn't be as she pretended to rock along with the music while really trying to grind herself against me.

Irritation spiked in my veins, the whiskey no longer doing its job as a dark yearning for more consumed me. Alyvia twisted around, the deep cleavage of her dress repulsing me more than anything else, before her ruby-red lips hovered near mine and then landed.

I didn't do anything, frozen on the spot as this

desperate woman writhed around me, doing her damnedest to seduce me like a Venus flytrap. There was nothing wholesome or sweet about her, and maybe that's why I fucking liked it.

Adrenaline launched through my system as I sank a hand into her loose waves of dark hair and fisted, arching her neck to one side with enough force to triple the heartbeat at her throat. "You think that kind of shit turns me on?"

Her fingers whispered across my neck, eyes trained on mine as she nearly melted under my hard gaze.

"It's gonna take a helluva lot more than that to get my dick hard." I released her, wishing she'd just fucking beat it, leave me to the whiskey and music, but I guessed like attracted like, and I was nothing if not desperate that night.

"Give me a chance?" Her lips touched mine again, leaving some sticky gloss that pissed me off even more. "I can make you feel better."

My cock finally did throb then, the promise of feeling better a bittersweet one.

Alyvia with an A, *and a Y,* slithered down under the table, red-tipped nails scratching along the zipper of my jeans as a faux-pout tilted her lips.

Bile rose in my throat.

She adjusted her tits in her dress, no doubt making sure I had a good view, which I did, before she pushed my knees apart and settled between them, huddled on the dirty floor under the table, eyes trying to seduce me.

To play this game with her.

To do the dance where we looked for love in all the wrong places.

I swallowed another painful knife, thinkin' nothing about this woman, or any woman, would be satisfying to me ever again.

Not after her.

Not after my whiskey girl.

She'd left her mark, inked deeper than any tattoo on my fucking soul.

The only woman's love I wanted, hell, needed—would *ever* need—was Augusta Belle's.

Just as the chick with the faux-pout was about to tackle the buckle of my belt, I shot out of the booth, careful not to hurt her as I pulled her up off the floor, helping her straighten her dress for a minute before cupping her face with my palm, "You're better than that. We both are."

And before she could throw her drink all over me, I was halfway across the bar, aiming for the cool night air of Jackson and the hotel where my girl was waiting, cuddled up in bed. Where I could hold her and be the man I should have been a few hours ago.

Shame and guilt ate me up on the few blocks back to the hotel, but I'd had some sort of fucked-up realization in that bar.

I'd take what Augusta Belle and I had on our worst days over any kind of shit I could have with anyone else.

There was no one else.

Never had been.

I'd been loyal from the start, and truth be told, I'd only been devastated at the thought of her keeping something from me for so long when I'd been an open book with her. I'd never had a thing to hide, but that didn't mean she didn't hold things close to her heart for her own reasons. That didn't mean I had a right to take those things away just because I wanted them. Just because I thought I was ready. If anyone knew me better than I did, it was Augusta Belle Branson, and if she was keeping something close, there was probably a reason for it.

I pushed through the doors of the hotel, nodding at the midnight porter as I strode through the lobby, the bittersweet taste the whiskey left on my tongue only made worse when I reached the door of our room, tapping once before waving the keycard and stepping in.

The room was dark.

Every corner silent.

I flicked on the light, striding to the bathroom to find it empty.

My eyes did a quick scan, noticing for the first time that her backpack was gone.

"Fuck," I breathed, eyes wild as I cast around the

room for my keys.

I'd left them on the table near the bed, and now they were gone, replaced by a single note.

Fuck off, Fallon.

"Ah Christ!" I spat, crumpling the note and shoving it down deep in my pocket.

I pushed a hand through my hair, anxiety rocketing up my throat as I slammed through the door and stomped down the hallway, not taking time to wait for the elevator before I bounded down the stairs three at a time.

I reached the lobby, calling across to the porter, "You see a girl leave in a big white truck?"

The porter only grinned, eyes bright as I approached. "She told me you'd ask that, sir."

I nodded, eyes widening at the knowledge that Augusta Belle had planned this escape ahead of time. "And?"

He grinned again, giving a nonchalant shrug before replying, "She said I shouldn't tell you a goddamn thing —her words not mine, 'course."

Anger pummeled through my muscles, my fists clenched as a roar fought its way out of my chest. "She took my fucking truck!"

"She said you'd be mad, said you'd look really scary, and that even if you start cussin', I shouldn't tell you."

"Oh, for fuck's sake!" I exclaimed, stalking off across the lobby toward the doors, first light of dawn cracking the horizon in the distance. "You gotta tell me where she's at, bro. I'll lose my fucking mind without her. I fucked up, I fucked up bad, and I went out and did some shit I shouldn't have done. I shoulda been there and held her while she fucking cried, but I couldn't do it. I wasn't strong enough then, but I am now, man. I swear to fuck, I am now. Just those few hours without her…" I pushed a hand over my eyes, the idea that I'd lost her for good this time finally settling in. "I can't fucking go through losing her again. You've got to understand." I was back in his face, eyes locking with his. "I love her."

His eyes flared, a triumphant grin lighting up his entire face. "Ah, she did tell me if you said that, I could tell you."

My eyes grew wider than fucking crop circles. "She left you with a fucking magic password?"

He nodded, pride growing like he'd actually won, and held up three fingers. "Three of them."

"Christ." I shook my head. "Where did she go? Dawn is our special time a'day, and this morning… Well, I've got somethin' to ask her."

A silly smile bubbled out of him before he pointed out the front door. "She's just across the street. Came down here cryin', and my wife loves a new face to chat with, so she brought her home to our house last night for homemade blueberry pie and sweet tea."

I tilted my head, squinting across the road to the

neighborhood of tiny houses he pointed to. "She's been at your house this entire time?"

He nodded proudly.

"Fuck, well, all right then. Thanks for helping her, I guess."

"You want to see her?" he asked.

"Uh…" I wasn't really sure what sorta territory I was in now. "I would."

He nodded. "My wife is probably already up. She starts her days early, likes to have hot cakes and fresh syrup waitin' for me when I get off the night shift."

"She sounds sweet." I indulged him.

"She is." He walked around the desk, gesturing me toward the door. "She wasn't always, but me either. We hung in together, though. Grew up alongside one another. Did my best to hold her in the dark times, and there were a lot of them. Lost our first son to tuberculosis when he was just a baby."

His admission rocked me, a wave of emotion pushing at my eyelids. "Sorry to hear that."

"But life goes on. Best you can hope for is someone easy to talk to, to share the days with." He patted me on the shoulder as he pushed open the door, pointing me across the street. "Little yellow house on the corner. Just walk on in, I'm sure she's expectin' ya."

And in that moment, it felt like I'd overcome a mountain of shame to get here, thankful for the old man watchin' out for my girl, honored he'd opened up even a little to me, a fucked-up roadie musician who couldn't even be tall enough to stand for his woman when she needed him most.

I sucked in a cool breath of morning air, nodding at him once before walking off across the parking lot and to the little yellow house on the corner that held my future.

I was finally gonna be strong enough to stand up for it.

And finally, without the whiskey, a soothing tingle ran through my blood.

I was gonna get my whiskey girl.

TWENTY-FOUR

Fallon

"Do you think I have a single word to say to you, Fallon Gentry?" Augusta Belle stood in the doorway of the little yellow house on a corner in Jackson, Mississippi, hands on her hips and directing all that anger at me.

I sobered up real quick in that instant. "The fact that you didn't take my truck and head home to leave me to fend for myself down here makes me think you might."

Her little fist clutched at the door, polka-dot shorts and tank top doing nothing to intimidate me like she probably wanted. "Woulda taken off in a second, but that woulda been grand theft auto, and I just don't have time for that."

I swallowed the bark of laughter, knowing she'd lay into me real good if I mocked her now.

I pushed aside the urge to haul her into my arms and hug her so damn tight my chest ached, but I'd have to smooth this one over first.

And I had a helluva lot of smoothing to do.

"Old guy across the street said something 'bout hot cakes and sweet tea." I stepped a tad closer, itching to run my fingers along the inside of her arm, feel her shiver underneath me, her lips quivering against mine.

It'd only been a few hours, and I missed her like it'd been the better part of a lifetime.

"Nothin' here for you. Now that you're sober, you can take your keys. Ms. Kathy's already offered to bring me to the bus station at nine."

"Hell if I'm letting you go home on a bus," I gritted out, fingers twitching as I reached out, catching her wrist, a silent request for her to hear me out. "I'll drive you home myself if that's where you wanna go, Augusta Belle. I'd drive you to the ends of the earth if that'd make you happy." I stepped even closer, swallowing the last bit of distance between us. "Call me crazy, but I don't think that's what you're lookin' for, though."

I traced a fingertip down her hairline, thumb grazing the arch of her cheekbone as her eyes drifted closed.

"Just give me a chance to show you how much you mean to me. I want to talk, really talk. I never was worthy of you, Augusta Belle, but the day we met, you wrapped yourself around my soul. The days you weren't

209

there it felt like a vise, squeezing all the life out of me. But the days I'm with you are the only days I feel the sunshine."

Tears tracked down her cheeks, wetting my hands and her shirt, soaking into my beard and making my chest hurt somethin' fierce.

I'd never known pain to exist outside of my body, but with Augusta Belle walkin' around in the world, it felt like an exposed nerve, my heart always on guard and vulnerable, ready to defend my love for her at any possible second.

"The world is hard. I've known that since the time I was old enough to string a sentence together, but then I had you. You came along and brought the sunshine." I thumbed away fresh tears, her finally wrapping her arms around my waist as she emptied her pain into my embrace. "I can drown myself in all the whiskey in Mississippi, but a man still needs his sunshine."

Her fingertips worked at the thin threads of my T-shirt, chest racked with waves of devastating pain.

I stood there.

I took it all.

I cried real tears with her on that front porch; I felt every horrifying moment of that night our baby was stolen from her deep in my bones.

She'd needed me then, and I wasn't there.

If I woulda been the man I was aimin' to be now, I

woulda hunted her down the day I knew she turned eighteen. I would have searched every college campus east of the Mississippi, then gone west if that's what it took.

And maybe, deep down, that's what I had been doin' all these years on the road.

Lookin' for my whiskey girl.

"Whaddya say we take the day? Explore Jackson?" I sank my nose into her hair, sucking in that sunshine and honey scent like my life depended on it.

"I'm still mad at you, Gentry," she sobbed, scrunching my shirt up in her little fists.

"Then I've got a lot of making up to do."

TWENTY-FIVE

Augusta

I twisted my hands in my lap, feeling a million miles away from Fallon even though he sat just across the cab of the truck, bench seat stretching lonely between us.

I'd gotten used to sittin' at Fallon's shoulder. The reassuring brush of his thigh, the stray touch of his fingertips against my knee something I'd come to live for, but that didn't change the last twelve hours.

Not in the slightest.

Him disappearin' just when I'd laid out my most precious secret? How could I be sure that wouldn't happen again when I said something he didn't like?

I'd held off divulging everything to him for that very reason, afraid I'd have to watch his back, walkin' away again.

My eyes held fast on the horizon, truck cruisin' down an old country road, lush green fields highlighted with the occasional stand of magnolia trees for almost as far as the eye could see.

"I don't remember Mississippi bein' quite so…pretty the last time I was here."

Fallon's eyes cut across the space between us, fingers twitching on the wheel. "Hard to see the nice things when you're blinded by heartache."

I let his words hang heavy, realizing how true they were on more levels than I could count.

"Y'know," he finally said, interrupting the silence, "Every day, every gig, no matter where I was, in a sea of people, my eyes never stopped searching for you."

A new ball of locked-up emotion threatened to overwhelm me before I swallowed it down, the reality that he'd ached as much as I had all those years like a fresh wound.

Fallon slowed the truck, sensing everything that still sat unsteady between us, turning into the first pull-off he could find.

I gnawed on my bottom lip as the shade of an ancient stand of magnolias draped in moss nearly swallowed us from the side of the road.

I opened the door to find the palest pink and white petals floating on the breeze, dancing onto the hood of Fallon's truck, landing in my hair, carpeting the soft dirt under my feet.

"It's a little like a fairy tale." I pushed the door closed behind me, coming around the front of the truck and meeting Fallon.

I felt his eyes on me, my only focus on the sweetly scented blooms engulfing us.

"Every day with you is a fairy tale, Augusta Belle." He followed at my shoulder as I waited at the base of one of the tallest trees in the grove, a pond riddled with moss-covered stone at the base. "I can't promise I won't fuck up. I have a bad habit of fallin' just when I need to stand tall, but I'm serious when I say that ends now."

His rough palms cupped mine, the gravelly lilt to his voice conveying the emotion he had trouble expressin' with words.

"Fucked up last night, I'm not proud. Wouldn't be right if I didn't tell you that I almost made the mistake of my life last night. Took almost losing it to see the beauty right in front of my face. With you. Even when it's hard, it's still so much more fucking perfect than I've ever had." His thumb caressed the sensitive hollow at my neck, eyes clinging to mine as if his life were at stake.

"What I did last night—" he squeezed his eyes closed "—reminded me of all those dark fucking nights I spent without you, looking for happy at the bottom of a bottle. Took till bein' with you again to remember that I'm not him. I'm the man I am when I'm with you, making

214

music, singing alongside you…" His head dipped, voice lowered. "…takin' care of you.

"I don't plan on ever bein' that man again. Took a flashback of it last night to send me runnin' the other way."

Both his arms encircled me then, holding me against his tall body, swallowing me against his form, sheltering me in him.

Right where I loved to be.

He hummed against my ear, swaying me softly as the wind swirled a cascade of blooms around us, the words of the song he'd been working on at my ear.

My rough and rowdy days long gone
You rode the storm and broke the chains
Rain clouds clear and the sunshine came
Aw, you kiss me sweet like honey and whiskey

Your love is warmer than sunshine and whiskey
Your love heats like honey and whiskey
Your love is sunshine and whiskey

We stood like that, heartbeats syncing as the harsh world faded at the edges.

As long as we could do this, everything would be okay.

I'd always felt that way about Fallon, and that feeling only grew with each passing memory we made.

"Sometimes I wish we had a second chance to meet again for the first time." He brushed his lips against mine, tingles spiraling through every piece of me with his touch. "Don't know what I would do different, but I'd find a way to do somethin'."

"I was fifteen, Fallon." I said the words softly, the inevitability of our outcome settling like a cloud. "There wasn't a thing else we coulda done."

He breathed against me, chest pressed against mine as one hand sank into the waves of my hair, lips finally touching mine in the tenderest of kisses.

Soft and slow, reflective and redemptive, our touch healed what our words couldn't.

TWENTY-SIX

Fallon

"Lived too many long days and dark nights without you, sunshine. We've got a past that neither one of us can help. But you and I have a say in our future, Augusta Belle. And I swear I'll spend every day of the rest of my life making it up to you." I held her fingers at my lips, leaving kisses over every tender spot.

Her eyes softened, hands wrapping around my neck when my palms cupped her thighs and I pulled her up against my waist, back pressed against the smooth bark of a giant magnolia. She locked her ankles around me, arms held so tight I thought she might suffocate me. And still, I didn't care, not as long as we were together.

"I love you. That never changed, I was just too stubborn to admit it before now. Marry me, Augusta

218

Belle. Please. Make me the happiest motherfucker south of the Mason-Dixon and be my wife."

Fresh sobs racked her form, a brilliant and toothy smile splitting her gorgeous face before she cried harder against my lips.

"Next town we're in, we can go anywhere you want and pick out a ring."

"Shut up." She held my face in her palms, peppering my lips with kisses. "I don't need a ring." She wove her fingertips into my hair, lips whispering against the sensitive skin at my neck. "But I do need something else."

I slid her down to her feet, soft pink light showering my girl in a radiant golden hue. "Anything."

"Sure about that?" A slightly scary twinkle lit her eyes for the first time in hours.

Christ, I'd do anything to keep that amused little glimmer in her eyes every day. "What did I just promise to do?"

"Well, first, you have to understand one thing." She held up a finger. "I didn't tell you, not because I wanted to hide anything, but because I had to be sure you were ready."

"Ready?" I arched an eyebrow.

Her grin faltered for an instant before she rested both of her hands on my forearms, pressing her lips together in thought.

"There's no other way to say this except that… Well, that name my dad left on the note. It kept eating at me, and then I went digging the night before I left to come see you. And I found—" She pulled a little chain from around her neck, a cameo dangling I hadn't noticed earlier. One I hadn't seen in more than a decade.

"The necklace I gave you," I breathed, shocked to see her wearing it now.

"I found it in an envelope, buried in the same folder as the rest of the other stuff about the fire and your dad'. And then there was this letter." She stopped, eyes haunted. "One letter."

"A letter?" I wasn't sure I was ready for the contents.

"And the only thing that was folded inside the letter was this picture." She slid a wallet-sized picture my way of a chubby, smiling baby, thighs the size of drumsticks and a shock of wild golden hair.

"Christ." I held the faded picture in trembling hands.

"A boy."

Silent tears swam in her eyes as she stepped closer, hand at my arm again. "I think it's him."

The earth about fell out from under my feet right then.

Him.

Augusta and I had a son.

Our little boy was out there somewhere.

How the fuck hadn't it occurred to me that we could

maybe find him? Meet him?

"Jesus," I breathed, handing the picture back as my heart clawed its way out of my throat.

"I had these big plans, so much hope when I was at the school that last month. I thought I would raise enough money for the bus fare back to Tennessee and find you, and then we could find him together. I never signed anything, Fallon. I never said they could give our baby up for adoption. They just took him."

I nodded, processing the overwhelming information cycling through my system.

"One of the nurses finally told me the baby needed that family more than he needed me, and I realized"— she was talking faster now, emotion clogging her words —"she was right. I couldn't be anything to him. And I heard so many stories of you in Nashville. I knew…well, I knew we would be nothing but trouble for that baby." She swallowed down more tears. "After I gave birth, the only thing anyone ever said that even acknowledged I'd had a baby was when the nurse finally whispered that the baby had 'gone to a good and godly family.'"

Her fingers trembled as she worked at the frayed hem of my shirt, distracting herself as she spilled everything she'd been carrying on her slim shoulders.

"So when I finally graduated high school, the counselor lined up a summer internship at Ohio State. They were the only school still accepting applications, and I thought the farther away I was, the easier I could forget. But at night… The nights used to get to me. The girls in my dorm would wake me up throwing pillows because I would just be crying in my sleep. By the end of the semester, they all knew I'd lost a baby, and they all requested to be transferred to a different floor. It was so hard. And not even knowing, not being able to see the sweet little person our baby was growing into…"

"Jesus, Augusta, you think that name your dad had written down might be connected to the people who adopted our boy?"

Wet eyelashes framed her big whiskey eyes as she gazed at me with new intensity. "I don't think so—I know so."

"And this is the thing you need? To find him?"

She paused, long, quiet beats more deafening than any sound could be.

A thousand thoughts rushed through my head, knowing every one she'd probably already had. She'd had years to process all of this. I had a lot of catching up to do, but the idea that our kid still might be better off without either of us in his life was at the forefront. Sometimes fate had a way of throwing a person only what they could handle. I liked to believe that most days, but Augusta's tears had me thinkin' somethin' else entirely.

"I have to know," she finally confessed, arms wrapping

around herself before I untangled her, pulling her into my arms for long minutes. My chin resting on her shoulder, I held her as her fingers clutched at my shirt and our minds ran away with us.

"I'll do anything it takes to make you feel better," I whispered against her sun-kissed hair.

She didn't reply for a long time, words caught in her throat before she breathed, "Thank you."

I nodded, rubbing her back and sensing on a primal level this woman needed to know what happened to the sun and stars that were stolen from her universe so many years ago. I understood she'd carried a burden I would never fully understand, nor could anyone else.

I'd do anything it took to help her find the missing piece.

"So, what's our first step? Researching that name?"

Augusta Belle pulled away, a soft smile turning up her lips as she wiped at the wetness covering her cheeks. "Well…"

"You've already done the research, haven't you?" I knew her, knew she wouldn't have been able to let it go once she had a name.

Her face lit for an instant, fingers working the little cameo at her neck back and forth.

"Don't tell me you found him?"

Her grin grew impossibly wider. "When I Googled that name, the only thing that came up was someone livin' in Landry, Mississippi."

My eyebrows shot up, realizing he could still be right here in this state.

"That's not far from the school I was at, Fallon. I think he's still right here."

I pulled her face into my hands, training my eyes on hers, looking…for what I wasn't sure. "You really think so?"

She nodded quickly, happy smile pulling at her lips.

"I think I found our boy."

TWENTY-SEVEN

Fallon

"Sasquatch could step out at any moment, and I wouldn't be at all surprised." I turned onto Old Biloxi road, more than three hours beyond Jackson, dense old-growth forest as far as the eye could see. Not creepy at all.

That's what I kept repeating to myself anyway.

"This is exactly what it looked like at the school I was at. I bet we're not far away," she mused from beside me, thighs pressed side by side, just like we'd been since the moment we'd gotten into my truck to take this journey.

561 Lucedale Court

Landry, MS

I'd memorized the address on the back of that envelope miles ago, my mind conjuring what a eight-

226

year-old boy one-part me, one-part Augusta Belle might look like.

Blond and freckled, if I had to guess.

"Would you ever wanna visit?"

"Sacred Heart?" she asked at my side with a shrug, "I looked it up ages ago. It closed. Not a single word about adoptions anywhere I could find, but they'd probably been hiding that aspect for years." Two fingers absentmindedly worked at the seam of my jeans. "Can't believe all this time he was right here. I should have come looking for him before now, but I think I…" She paused, glancing over at me, "I think I needed you first."

I pushed a hand into the wild mess of her hair, pulling her to me for a soft kiss at the crown of her head. "I'm glad you waited. You rocked my world, but I wouldn't change a second of it."

"You drive me crazier than you ever did before, there's no doubt about that." She pinched my thigh, featherlight giggle filling up all four dark chambers of my heart. "I know I'm crazy for wanting to do this, I know it. I haven't even thought about what we should do when we get to town. Try to track down a phone number? Just show up at that address and pray they still live there? Oh, and aren't they going to kick us off their property the second after we arrive?"

I heaved a deep breath, pulling her in closer, tryin' to squeeze out some of that anxiety that had her so worked up. "You're cute as a button when you're all wound up, Augusta Belle, but we can't worry 'bout any of that till we get there. And to be honest, it's comin' up on dark, and I'm worried if there's even gonna be a hotel in good ole Landry."

Her eyes grew wide as hubcaps before she burst into laughter. "There is, worrywart. I'm already one step ahead of you. Checked my phone last night after you walked out. There's a few good swimming holes too." Her eyes crinkled as she laughed. "Thought 'bout drivin' to Landry myself, but I didn't have the heart to leave you all alone in Jackson."

"Kind of you," I quipped. "And glad to hear you did some recon on Landry."

She shrugged, digging into her backpack and pulling out the envelope with the address for no less than the dozenth time, sliding out the old, worn picture, the little boy's chubby cheeks rosy and round, so sweet I could almost hear the giggle in his voice.

She propped the picture up on the dashboard, head turning to the side as she smiled and rubbed at my knee through navy denim.

"Think you want more kids someday?" I ventured.

Her smile faded, and the fingers working back and forth at my leg paused. "I hope."

"Can't imagine a better mama," I said, meaning it with every bone.

Maybe we weren't meant to be parents again right now, but that could change in an instant.

I could buy us a place, any old place she wanted, and we could start a family.

I'd do that for her, without hesitation.

"I don't have a great example, can't imagine what it's like to have a healthy parent-child relationship. I don't know if it's something I'd be good at at all, but yeah." She twisted up her smile again. "I think I'd like to."

I was still thinkin' 'bout babies and Augusta Belle when an old rusted-up roadside sign declared Landry five miles ahead.

Her eyes cast across the space between us, my own smile cresting up as unspoken words slipped between us.

This was it.

I pulled into the first parking lot that displayed a vacancy sign, a roadside motel that looked out of another age but recently and cheaply remodeled.

"Gettin' late. Figure we shouldn't go surprisin' anyone this time a'night. Get a good night's rest, and then we can tackle our next step in the morning?"

She nodded, hopping out of the truck and straight into my arms. I cupped her round bottom in my hands as she kissed me like she'd been achin' to do it 'bout as long as I had.

"I like this frisky side of you," I whispered between kisses, shuttin' the door of my truck with the back of my boot and walkin' with her in my arms right through the tiny lobby of the hotel.

The night manager raised an eyebrow before uttering, "How many nights?"

"Not sure yet," I said, finally lowering my girl and clutching her hand in mine. "We'll start with a week, I guess."

He huffed, punching a few things into the ancient desktop before sliding a keycard across the counter. "We'll need a card to hold the room."

"Right." I nodded, digging into my wallet and sliding out a credit card for him. "Hey, any dive bars nearby?"

Augusta Belle stifled a giggle at my side.

"Down on the corner, past the 7-Eleven." His voice was so monotone, I almost asked if he'd had that question before.

"Room 6, out the front doors, down to the right. Gave you a room with a view. You're welcome."

I nearly laughed, but instead, thanked him, grabbing on to Augusta and heading back out the way we'd come. Turning a sharp right, I headed down the concrete sidewalk until we reached the last room at the end.

"Guess he meant a view of the cornfield." Augusta Belle dumped her backpack on the surprisingly clean king bed and kicked off her shoes.

She looked gorgeous, and while my stomach was rumbling for food, something was telling me a taste of her would satisfy me even more.

"The bathtub is huge!" she called from the corner bathroom. I heard the water then, steam filling the room moments later. I leaned against the doorframe, watching her for a moment as she tested the water with her hand before shedding the T-shirt over her head.

I stifled a groan before going to her, lips kissing along the soft shell of her ear, down the line of her neck, over the bare skin of her shoulders before slipping a finger under the strap of her black bra. "May I?"

She nodded, eyes falling closed as a soft little puff of air fell from her lips.

I pushed the bra straps off her shoulders, seeing a spray of goose bumps in my wake as her breathing kicked up.

"You're the most gorgeous—" I murmured, unhooking the snaps of her bra "—stubborn—" the straps fell, only her hands cupping her breasts "—intoxicating woman I've ever met."

I worked my hands around the front of her waist, unhooking the button and pulling down the zipper of her jeans, pushing them into a heap on the floor. She stepped out of them, and I trailed my nose back up the silk of her inner calf. I brushed my fingernails at the underside of her knee as I glided my lips up the outer curve of her succulent thighs, the hum of her arousal growing with each pass of my lips. I sucked in a breath, nose filled with the heady scent of her body, aching for the thing that'd been missing between us, that pulsing undercurrent we couldn't seem to escape.

"Are you sure you're ready for this, Augusta Belle?" I skated my fingers across the waistband of her panties.

She nodded fiercely, fingertips digging into my shoulder blades. "Please?"

I hugged her waist, nipping at the elastic with my teeth and snapping it against her sweet flesh, the soft jerk of her hips against my face enough to do me in alone. "Christ, I can smell how turned on you are."

My mouth watered, palms moving passed the vee at her thighs and over the soft flesh of her belly, tongue dancing around the concave indentation of her navel before continuing up.

With her wrists in both of my hands, I worked them over with soft nips and kisses before darting my tongue out to trace the outline of her peaked nipple.

She sucked in a violent breath, moan breathing past her lips before one of her hands was in my hair and she was inching closer.

"More."

I groaned, arousal dampening the front of my jeans as my cock bit into the hard metal of my zipper, alive and ready to be home for the first time in years.

"Augusta Belle…" My control wore thin, her whiskey-hued irises trained on mine. "Never thought we'd find ourselves here again." I pushed one palm up the curve of her delicate neck and into the wild mass of waves. "Never thought I'd find home again." I moved up her body, pressing her lips to mine in a kiss that conveyed so much more than I could put into words. "But home ain't a place," I whispered against her ear, "it's inside you.

"I'll keep asking you to marry me until I get the answer I want, Augusta Belle." My other palm worked at her breast, sliding rough thumbs against her nipples and then caressing away the pain. "But I hope you're prepared for a helluva lotta persuadin' on my part."

I pushed both her breasts together in my palms, coaxing the delicious flesh into my mouth and eliciting another groan, this one deeper, from somewhere primal, out of her mouth.

One of her palms pushed between us, working the buttonhole on my jeans before I grew impatient and slipped the button free and discarded them on the floor. The only thing separating us was thin undergarments. Hot, damp skin waiting to come together in a reunion of need before this thing between us imploded, causing greater destruction.

"You on any sorta birth control?" I braced myself for her answer, but I found the unexpected when she locked eyes with me and shook her head.

"Never had a reason to."

"I figured you'd moved on…" I pushed a hand down

into the waistband at the back of her panties, dusting at the round flesh of her behind.

"I wanted to." Her fingertips worked across my pectorals, fingernails tracing ink I'd collected over my years on the road. Half the tattoos I had I'd be hard-pressed to remember the entirety of the night I'd gotten them, but maybe that was part of the experience.

"But I never could." She pushed her lips against mine, my control spiraling until I pushed her panties and my boxers down and carried us both into the jetted tub that bubbled and boiled.

I sank down into the bubbles, and she cradled herself against my form, rocking in slow, sweet motion as I slid through the hot seam of her body. I pushed at the entrance before some sort of familiar puzzle piece locked into place, and suddenly I was sinking slowly inside her, our mouths connected as hands trailed up and down skin, gasps of breath the only thing separating us before we were sliding together and falling deeper.

My hands traced the curve of her spine, her hands in my hair as we kissed and rocked, my body rooting itself down deep in the only happiness I'd ever known.

With this woman, I could lose control.

With this woman, I could be me—right here, in the now.

"Fallon," she hummed, body spasming as a slow shudder of arousal sent waves of ecstasy climbing up my spine.

"I'm here. I've always been right here." I placed a hand over her hammering heart. "You took my heart with you when you left, Augusta Belle. Had it stashed safely away this whole time until we could come together again."

Her eyes flared with overpowering emotion, cupping my face with her hands before our lips connected and she showed me she was feelin' exactly the same sorta way I was. "I love you, Fallon."

Working the pads of my fingers between us, I found the hot little bundle of nerves that sent her eyes rolling, neck arching, fingernails digging into my shoulders as spasm after spasm of decadent pleasure overtook her.

I watched riveted, hopeless when my own release pummeled through every nerve of my body. Our slick skin moving together was the soundtrack to our love before our hearts were the only bass line we heard, our bodies melding together as the water and the bubbles eased away the outside world, our own bubble growing as my hands traced her skin, her lips working against mine, our souls refusing to let go of the solace we'd finally found.

Drunk on each other.

TWENTY-EIGHT

Fallon

"Mmm, mornin', sunshine."

She was sitting atop a picnic table, bathed in beautiful morning light, notebook spread in her lap.

"Mornin', Gentry." She flicked her eyes up, shining with somethin' so brilliant I couldn't help but be a little blinded.

"Looks like someone had a good night." I plopped myself on the warm wood beside her, enjoying the way being in the sun and her presence made somethin' deep inside me warm from the core out.

Augusta Belle had a light so bright, not even life's darkest days could dim her.

Hell, maybe that's the thing I loved about her most.

Or more likely, it was just one in a long line of things

that made me hers.

I might pretend to be six foot five and bulletproof, but the woman I'd found tryin' to leap off the Whiskey River Bridge that day so many years ago could bring me to my knees with just a look.

"I actually had the best night ever, thanks to this growly Southern rocker guy I know."

I barked a laugh, hauling her into my lap and letting the notebook fall onto the table between us. She worked her hips against mine, lips locking as her teeth caught my flesh and dragged. "He's the moodiest, sweetest, kindest soul I know, and I just have to make peace with the fact that he's way cooler than I am."

"Don't forget most talented," I offered, locking a hand in her hair and pulling her against my lips in a deeper kiss. "Never lettin' you go again, Augusta Belle. Not over my dead body."

"Good," she whispered, voice clogged with vulnerable emotion. "Because I don't think I could stand it again."

I swallowed, lifting her in my arms and carrying her right back through the French doors and into that king bed to show her how much I loved her all over again. Somethin' I'd never get sick of doin' for as long as I walked this earth.

Lovin' Augusta Belle came easier than breathin'.

* * *

By the time her tummy was rumbling a few hours

later, we were both freshly showered and changed, prepared to drop off a load of clothes with the dry cleaner, my preferred method of doing laundry since the day I started livin' out of my truck, and then we had plans to visit the address printed on that envelope.

Lucedale Court.

Augusta Belle had searched for a phone number, but after half a dozen failed calls and countless no-answers, we decided the only other option we had was to knock on doors.

Augusta Belle's hand gripped mine after we'd slid out of the truck, eyes peering up at the big house ahead of us. "You think this is it?"

"Tire swing in the yard, baseball bat…" I mused, eyes taking in the otherwise tidy front lawn. "Looks like a boy lives here."

"The neighborhood is great," she murmured, both of our gazes taking in the elegant colonials that lined the quiet neighborhood street. "Maybe we should just leave this. Look, it may not even be him, and what could we possibly say to make any sort of sense of what happened?" She looked up, eyes terrified and trained on mine.

I squeezed her hand, trying to lend her the small sense of calm I had at this moment. "We'll do our best."

Our gazes held, a dozen years of history shrouding our shoulders as we stepped up the sidewalk, headed to the stately front doors, hearts in our throats.

She gnawed on her bottom lip when I tried the knocker and waited.

Nothing.

Silence.

Stifling silence.

I was about to lift a hand to the doorbell when the soft click of a lock sounded and the door cracked open.

"'Allo?"

"Hi, my name is Augusta Belle Branson. Do you by chance know anyone by the name of Victoria Hill?"

I watched, riveted. The gentleman standing behind the door was slim, a sort of worried look crossing his features.

"She doesn't live here anymore," he muttered, closing the door.

"Wait!" Augusta Belle pressed both her hands to the worn wood, eyes wild as she tried to peek into the window that decorated the top.

I knocked again, calling calmly, "We'd just like to ask a quick question. We're not even sure if she's who we're looking for, but if you could just hear us out for a minute —"

The door cracked open again, haunted, dark eyes lingering on us before he opened the door a little farther, stretching to his full height and taking a deep breath. "Victoria Hill was my wife. She's gone now." He swallowed, and I sensed something painful had hit this family. "An accident last year."

"I'm so sorry for your loss," I offered. "I guess there's no easy way to say this, but Augusta Belle here found a folder with some important information, your wife's name the only thing pointing us in this direction."

"What is it you're lookin' for, exactly?" He crossed his arms, patience seeming to wear thin already.

Augusta Belle stepped forward, straightening her own spine before locking eyes with the man. "I had a baby at a place named Our Lady of Sacred Heart, and that baby was adopted. That was nine years ago."

The instant the word was out of her mouth, his eyes fell, turning to a look of defeat before his shoulders slumped and he stepped aside, door opening up to a simple entryway beyond. "I knew this day would come."

"Oh my God," Augusta Belle murmured, stepping into the entry to see a framed school photo of a little boy, his smile subtle, eyes twinkling with mischief, and a spray of freckles across his cheeks.

He was gorgeous.

"Is this him?" she asked, fingertips hovering just above the glass of the photo, tears welling in her eyes.

The man nodded. "Jack Christopher. He's at school now, but…" His eyes were trained on mine. "Maybe later we could arrange a meeting?"

"A meeting?" my girl whispered.

The guy shrugged. "Jack's been askin' about his birth parents for a while. We just didn't have a way of finding anything out about…" He paused, watching Augusta Belle as she moved down the hallway, devouring more photos of the little boy she'd loved and lost. "Met the kid's grandpa the night we picked up Jack. We asked him for anything he could tell us about the family, but he was so mum. Left us with an address to send updates, and we did, a few times, but never heard back. Figured the family wanted to move on…"

Augusta Belle's silent tears left trails of salt down her cheeks as she lingered at the same photo she'd found in her dad's attic—same chubby thighs and bright smile, only a larger version. "He looked like a happy baby."

"I'm sorry, guess I should introduce myself. I'm Calvin Hill." He thrust a hand out to me, and I shook it. "Jack was such a happy baby. We tried for so long to have a baby, and then when he came along…" He glanced at Augusta Belle then back to me. "Well, he was so much more than we ever could have dreamed for." He swallowed, eyes landing on a family photo of the three of them, Jack a few years younger than he was now, smiling gleefully in his mother's arms. "Losing his mom was hard on him. He's struggled at school, just hasn't been quite the same. I've got some family that helps out when they can, but nothing can replace a mother's love." He halted, as if he'd said the wrong thing, when Augusta

Belle's gaze trained on him.

"I can't believe it was so easy. That all this time, he was right here…" She covered her face, and I pulled her into my arms, rubbing her back and trying to soothe away the long-buried ache.

"We offered, well, welcomed your dad and the whole family to come down and get to know Jack Christopher. Sacred Heart offered a closed adoption, but we were so happy that any baby was…available at all… Well, we woulda taken anything, I think."

Her eyes watered as she looked up at the man. "That night… You said my dad was there?"

He nodded. "We picked Jack up at Sacred Heart when he was three days old. Your father is the one who passed him into my arms."

"That's impossible. It must have been someone else. Dad never came to see me, never even mentioned the pregnancy. No one talked to me while I was there…"

The old guy shrugged. "Just a second." He held up a finger then disappeared into a hall closet, pulling out a folder of discolored papers. "I have something that may clear this up. Ah, there it is." He pulled out a Polaroid, handing it to me. And sure enough, there stood Augusta Belle's father, an infant in his arms wrapped in a little blue blanket, a tortured look in his eyes.

Jesus. Augusta Belle didn't even grab for the picture, just stared at it, eyes roaming over every inch before she buried her head in my arm and let out a fresh batch of tears.

"That's him." I handed the photo back.

"And you're the, ah, biological father?" he asked cautiously.

I nodded, holding back my own emotion.

I'd missed out on so much—the baseball games, the first day of school, swimming lessons, first steps, and giggles.

"Augusta, well, she's been dealing with a lot of the things that happened while she was at that place. She was taken against her will, as you can imagine. But beyond that, it seems…well, that school didn't have her sign anything about adopting her baby. She thought she was going to take him home to Tennessee and raise him herself…"

The man's eyes widened. "But I've got the paperwork right here, clearly has the signature of the mother listed." He pulled out another piece of paper, my eyes scanning it for Augusta Bell's flowery signature.

It was there, all right, but it certainly wasn't hers.

In fact, it looked like the signature of a sixty-year-old woman, controlled and precise. Augusta Belle's had always been all large loops and youthful feeling.

"You didn't sign that, did you, Augusta?" the older man finally asked, her eyes clear enough to see the signature that so obviously wasn't hers on Jack

Christopher's birth certificate.

"No."

He nodded, pushing a hand into his hair. "Look, I won't lie and say things since my wife passed have been great. Jack and I have had a lot of painful moments, but putting him through a legal battle now—"

"Oh my God, no. I would never." She was clutching at the stranger's hand now, the very stranger who'd raised our son. "We don't want to change his life at all. I guess I just needed… I guess I just needed to know that he was all right, taken care of, loved." She looked around the house, focusing on the pictures mostly. "And he is. I can tell he's gotten so much more here with you than I ever could have given him—"

"That's not true." Jack's dad looked from me to her. "Maybe at one time, we had it all. But I can't raise Jack alone and do it well." He pressed his lips together, assessing his next words. "He needs a mother, and I just can't be that for him." He looked up at me. "Don't know how long you planned on stayin' in town for, but while you're here, I'd love if you could spend time with him. I think he would love it. He's such a brilliant little guy, so advanced and beyond his age, asking the questions he's always asked. I think…I think talking to you would help him."

Augusta Belle's hand clutched at mine, hope springing into her eyes for the first time since we'd walked up.

"Really?"

"Absolutely." He nodded, setting the folder down on the table. "He won't be off the bus for a few hours yet. Whaddya say we sit down and chat a little more?"

She nodded, kicking off her shoes and following him down the long hallway before I could even think twice.

I followed suit, kicking off my own dirty boots and taking off down the tile hallway after them, visions of my boy's beautiful face wallpapering every surface as I went.

Augusta Belle had found our boy.

The son we hadn't even realized we had.

Evidence of the night that'd changed both of us.

The night we created him.

TWENTY-NINE

Augusta

My heart clenched, Jack and Fallon walking side by side down the length of the yard, heads tilted to the side in just the same way. "They're so much alike."

Jack's dad, Calvin, as he'd insisted we call him, nodded once, quiet smile playing on his lips. "They do. Answers a lot of questions. Like why Jack has such an ear for music, for one."

"Got that honestly," I said, heart finally easing into its place inside my own chest as I watched the son who was stolen from me walk next to the man who'd changed my life.

Saved my life.

Both of them had, in different ways.

I was still digesting the idea that my father had known

my son, held him if even for a few brief moments.

I had to bite back the resentment. But, in other ways, I think it made sense why he kept the things he kept. Maybe he thought he'd tell me someday how everything had happened.

Or maybe he even felt some remorse.

I had to believe he did, the mystery of why he'd left Fallon our family house not quite so startling.

I had to believe that my dad regretted how so many things were handled. Maybe he just didn't have the words to express that regret.

How easy was it, after all, to say sorry for stealing someone's life?

I wiped emotional tears from my eyelashes as Fallon and Jack paused at the edge of the yard, Fallon pointing up into the sky as a jet tracked across the puffy white clouds.

"We'd love it if you'd stay for dinner," Calvin said, standing up from his place in the lounge chair and hovering at the French doors separating us from the large kitchen.

I swallowed the ball of emotion in my throat and turned, eyes glimmering up at this man I'd only just met. "Yes, we would love that. Thank you so much. I can't even begin to express what you've given me today." Emotion crawled out of my throat, threatening to choke my words, but I pushed on. "You've given me life."

His soft smile turned up, a gentle nod before he pinched his own tears away. "I think you came just in time, Augusta. We need you more than you know."

I had to contain myself then, swallowing and covering my eyes as I held it together, not wanting to present the image of a crying lunatic on the very first day I met my son and his family for the first time.

I turned, eyes focusing back on my boys, now walking back slowly, lost in conversation as Jack began asking Fallon every question under the sun about playing guitar, writing songs, singing onstage, and making music.

"I'll teach ya, if you'd like." Fallon bent down to his level, one broad, tattooed hand resting on his little shoulder.

I wanted a snapshot of this movement, wanted to capture it in my mind and relive it a thousand times over, relishing in the happiness.

"I would love that." Jack's toothy grin stole my heart.

I stepped up to their tight little circle, bending to find myself at Jack's level, his warm bronze eyes smiling back at me. "If it's okay with you, we're gonna stay for dinner."

Jack nodded fiercely, blond locks of hair falling across his forehead. On instinct, I reached out, pushing it behind his ear before catching myself.

The sweet little boy was smiling back at me, innocent wonder as he took in everything.

This morning, he'd gone to school with a single dad. This afternoon, he came home to Fallon and me.

While it felt confusing and amazing to Fallon and me, Jack seemed to take it all in stride, his grin popping when his dad told him exactly who we were. He first asked where we lived, and then a cascade of questions had ensued as he'd sat riveted at the kitchen table.

"Come on, buddy. Let's go help your dad make dinner." Fallon patted our son on the back.

Jack scrunched up his face. "Dad doesn't make dinner. He'll probably just order pizza."

I raised an eyebrow, grinning as I found one more way I could be of use. "Well, let's change that. We can make dinner, can't we? What are you in the mood for?"

"Really?" Jack ran up the steps of the porch, waiting for us at the door. "Let's make cake!"

He launched into the kitchen, circling his arms around his dad's leg and announcing that I'd promised him we were makin' cake. "How 'bout we save that for after we make dinner?"

Calvin laughed, waving me off. "I'll just order in. Don't wanna waste your time."

"It's not a waste of time at all." I rubbed at Jack's back, savoring even the tiniest touch. "I'd love to make dinner for you, and I'd love it even more if you helped me, Jack."

He nodded, happy to help, before sliding across the

floor in his socks to snag a barstool, then pushing it back across the floor to prop next to the stove. "I'm ready to chef."

Fallon stifled a laugh, my own smile stretching the boundaries of my face.

My heart was on fire.

Just this little boy's existence gave me a reason to breathe. To have the chance to know him, to be in his life, was another gift entirely.

I didn't know how long Jack's dad would let Fallon and me get to know Jack, but for as long as he was willing, I would take it.

By the time Fallon and I left that night, our bellies were full of fried chicken and chocolate cake and sweet tea.

"He looks just like you," Fallon murmured once we'd slid into the cab of his truck.

"But the way he acts, his mannerisms, they're all you." My grin split my face, a tiny shriek finally vibrating from my throat. I clutched both of Fallon's hands in mine, wiggling in my spot at his side, heart threatening to leap right out of my chest and fly away from me.

"He's a great kid."

"With such a great life," I agreed, eyes turning up to the big house we'd just spent the better part of eight hours in.

"And Calvin is nice," Fallon commented, voice

lowering, mind losing itself in thoughts he wasn't going to share.

I fell silent, the engine of the truck starting up before Fallon eased away from the house that'd held all my hopes and dreams for so long. Moonlight glinted off the glittery Elvis keychain, the only thing I could bear to focus on as I thought about the next time I might see our son, how many more firsts I would miss.

A few sad and stubborn tears leaked out of my eyes before I halted them, refusing to dwell on the time I'd lost, trying my damnedest to live in this moment.

I cuddled a little closer to Fallon, his ability to be attuned to me so sharp that his hand fell on my leg on instinct, giving me a few warm and reassuring squeezes before settling there.

Something about being beside him, his big body eating up the space around me, making me feel so small and fragile in comparison ensured I felt safe, at home, protected, and loved.

Fallon had done nothing but love all the dark and scary parts of me from the beginning.

Even then, there'd been so much I was running away from, so much I was searching for, an aimless soul looking for an anchor.

"Thank you for bringing me here," I whispered, gratitude seeping through my body. "I never could have faced any of this without you. You were always the other piece of my past, the missing part I needed to put all of this together."

"I'll be at your side till the day I take my last breath, Augusta Belle. Whether you're ready for it or not."

I tucked in a little closer to the man who had given me so much life, every moment I was with him more inspiring, more fulfilled.

"I'm ready for more than you think I am."

THIRTY

Fallon

"So lemme get this straight. You actually won *awards…*for *swimming?*" Jack's wide cognac eyes grew as if the notion were downright unbelievable, beach towel under one arm as we walked the dirt path to Landry's only swimming hole.

"Bet your life, she did," I chimed in, winking at Augusta Belle.

We'd been in town for over two weeks now, the quarters at Landry's finest roadside motel becomin' a little cramped. But all the quality time with Jack well worth the squeeze.

And Augusta.

Every day since the one we'd had our reckoning under the magnolia trees somewhere between here and Jackson

254

had been as damn near close to perfect as any I'd had. Augusta just had that way of shakin' up things, enough adventure to keep you on your toes and pushin' for just a little more.

Augusta was my more.

Always had been.

I'd finally just gotten around to showin' her that, every moment I had with her.

And now we were blessed with Jack, the wildly hilarious, unbelievably sarcastic eight-year-old who seemed to be adjusting to his new extended family shockingly well.

Guess somethin' about the way Augusta and I came together all those years ago didn't surprise me that we'd created life. It'd felt like the earth had flipped upside down and inside out, my world never the same again.

The night we met like two stars, combustin' together in a perfect, beautiful storm not far from the banks of the Whiskey River.

"You wanna see a pro in action?" Augusta Belle's sweet twang pulled me from my memories.

"Bring it!" Jack called, dropping his towel as soon as the pathway opened up and running as fast as his legs could carry him to the edge of the river. He turned, giving us each a wave before jumping off the small ledge, landing in an almost belly flop, and then coming up for air, radiant grin on his face.

We all erupted into laughter, Augusta already pulling her shirt over her head and discarding it at my feet, rebel twinkle in her eyes. She climbed up the taller slab of stone, Jack's eyes the size of dinner plates as he watched her from water level.

A teenager launched himself headlong over the cliff and landed in a slow-moving whirlpool of river water below.

I gave Augusta two thumbs up when she reached the top of the stone, pulling her hair back into a ponytail before throwing both of us one last wave and an air kiss.

I sucked in a breath, the familiar sense of knots twisting in my stomach when she backed away from the edge, then sprinted on angel's wings across the hard stone, launching headfirst over the side and arching like a swan, fingertips reaching above her head as she free-fell.

Jack watched, eyes bigger than the tires on my truck when Augusta cut through the water, disappearing under the current. We both waited, his eyes on the spot she'd vanished, mine on him.

My beautiful boy.

The last week 'Jack had been in my life, he'd brought more sunshine than I knew I was missin', the thought of his absence becomin' harder to take.

I still didn't know what was next for Augusta Belle and me; we hadn't talked about it. I wasn't sure how I felt about things, but watchin' her be a mom to Jack was like watchin' a flower bloom after the first spring rain.

I couldn't take her away from that, but what opportunities Landry had for me I wasn't sure.

The thought of livin' far away from this kid left a dark cloud hangin' over my head, but I didn't know if it was darker than the idea of stayin' in Landry either.

I had some cash stashed, but I had no plans for retiring anytime soon.

Short of losing Augusta Belle, losing my lifeline—the music—sounded like another idea of hell.

But could I lose my boy?

Jack's eyes searched the still waters, worry lacing his features before Augusta surfaced just out of reach of him, hair soaked down the length of her back, triumphant smile on her face.

"Dude, how did you hold your breath that long?" Jack looked up at the woman who'd birthed him, displaying the same rebel twinkle, upturned nose dotted with a spray of sweet freckles, deep brown eyes, and honey hair.

There was no doubt on the planet that he was hers.

"You've just got to practice. Even a few minutes every day can help build your lung capacity, and that's the key to outracing the competition." She pushed a hand through his wet hair.

"Holding your breath?" He ducked away, splashing her as he did.

"Nope." She splashed him back. "Practicin'." She

splashed again, then turned, eyes set on me.

I held up my arms, shaking my head before she used both hands to paddle as much water my way as she could muster. Jack joined in, and before long, I was soaked to the core, pullin' off my shirt and divin' in after them. Jack laughed when I launched more water his way, before ducking and paddlin' away.

"That boy can swim too." I stopped as soon as he was out of earshot.

Augusta Belle snaked her arm around my waist, leaning her head against my chest as she sighed. "He's the sweetest, smartest, most sarcastic human I've ever met." She twined her fingers with mine. "Next to you."

I grinned, about to grace her forehead with a kiss when a tsunami from hell caught me by surprise and an evil little laugh cackled just out of my reach.

"He's definitely his mother's kid," I hummed under my breath before launching into the water and swimming toward Jack.

Augusta was hot on my tail, teaming up with Jack to soak me to the bones for the rest of the afternoon.

The very best time of my life.

* * *

"So, you're tellin' me I don't have any grandparents left?" Jack asked, dribbles of watermelon still dripping off his chin as we finished what was left of our picnic.

258

"Well…" Augusta put an arm around Jack, ruffling the short spikes of his new haircut, something "cool" for baseball, he'd requested. "Life can be unfair sometimes, buddy."

His eyes tracked from mine across the picnic table to Calvin's and then finally landed on Augusta's. "But I don't understand. Dad showed me that picture. I had a grandpa, he knew about me."

I swallowed the burn blazing a trail down my throat. I wished I had something to tell him, some consolation for the fact that sometimes people just weren't nice. That was all I could ever come up with to explain the awfulness of the world anyway.

"I don't know why he chose to do what he did, Jack," Augusta finally offered.

"I bet not a day went by he didn't regret it, son. And what have we always told you?" Calvin's eyes held steady on Jack's.

"That sometimes people just aren't ready to raise a baby," Jack recited.

I chewed on my bottom lip, wishing I had more to give. "It's true, Jack," I finally murmured. "Augusta Belle and I, well, we weren't in any place to have a baby. And maybe life coulda been different, but who's sayin' life woulda been any better if we had? I've spent a lot of my life wishin' I could change the past, and it was a lotta life wasted." I pressed a hand on his back. "I'm not about to waste any more of that time."

Jack frowned but nodded with reluctant understanding.

"The truth is"—Augusta's eyes bounced from Calvin's then to Jack—"my parents…*your grandparents*…well, I believe they thought they were doin' what was best." She knocked shoulders with our boy. "But I know for sure they wish they could be here now, watching you hit home runs with the Eagles and swimming like a star."

He turned up his face, eyes catching the sun and glowing. "I want to go to Tennessee someday, see the ridge, and the river you used to swim in. I want to see the house too."

My heart thrummed quicker with his words, the idea of bringing him home to Chickasaw, showin' him all those places that were the backdrop of Augusta's and my story… I didn't know if I had the heart to relive it all, especially through his young eyes.

"Maybe someday, pal." Augusta grinned. "How's about right now we clean up and then head downtown for some ice cream?"

"Can we, Dad?" Jack asked Calvin.

He nodded. "Home by dark, though. You've got one more day of school before the weekend."

"Ugh. Can't I stay with Fallon 'n' Augusta?" His little Southern drawl was more noticeable in the evening when he was tired. Reminded me of Augusta even more with that twang.

"We don't really have a good situation set up for sleepovers, buddy." Augusta glanced at Calvin. "That hotel is close, but there isn't much room…"

"I can sleep on the floor. I don't care!"

"That's definitely not happening," I announced, a little repulsed. "Maybe we could find something bigger to rent for the weekend?"

Calvin shook his head, patting Jack on the shoulder. "Maybe someday, buddy, but you best be movin' on that ice cream if you want to get there before they close."

Jack slipped his hand into Augusta's, her cheeks warming as a slow smile crossed her lips at his contact.

I sucked in a breath, thoughts of what the world held for us as we took off for the sidewalk, sights set on ice cream, my mind a blur with possibilities.

THIRTY-ONE

Augusta

Dawn light shone through the faded blinds of the motel window, my eyes fluttering open just as Fallon's heavy palm made contact with the sensitive underside of my knees. He dusted his nose along the edge, grazing my thigh before his teeth nipped at the waistband of my panties and yanked, eliciting a squeal from my lips.

"Mornin', sunshine. I'm hungry for breakfast, and I want all three courses between your thighs." He caged me in his arms, the gravelly timbre of his voice sending my stomach spiraling.

This man. His words.

He'd been undoing me from the start with his words.

I arched beneath him, his heavy hands roaming up my torso before one palm cupped at my breast, thumb tracing my nipple as he slipped the other hand down the back of my panties and pushed them down my cheeks.

"Sounds promising." I moaned, fingernails digging into his biceps as my heart hammered at a fever pitch, the rough sandpaper of his beard causing new and delicious sensations to rocket through my body.

"You don't even know the half of it." He locked his hands with mine, his body pushing its way down my torso, grating over every last delicious nerve, his effect on me spinning my head a little more out of control.

Lost in him.

I'd always been so utterly lost in this man.

"Spread those sweet knees, sunshine."

I did what he ordered, anticipation making me his captive.

With his hands holding mine at my sides, he locked me to his body, mouth spread over the juncture of my legs as he moved his tongue against my skin, eliciting moans and whimpers of pleasure with each stroke.

He pressed the palm of his hand against my hips, holding me to him as his mouth glided around my core, devouring me in deft sweeps and swallowing me whole. Tremors of overwhelming pleasure and pain blasted through my body, shaking me from the inside out, rendering me speechless and stunned.

Before I could even begin to imagine what was on his mind, he was lifting me in his arms, locking my ankles around his waist and sliding inside, filling me with measured strokes and caressing the sensitive hollows of my throat with his lips.

"More, Fallon. Please more."

He clutched at my back, angling his hips deeper, creating a new rhythm as we connected, rocking together, wrapped around each other limb for limb, life for life.

"You don't know what it does to me, knowin' all those desperate little whimpers are mine." His rough beard skated across my breasts, my nipples tightening as our skin grew damp, the only noise what our bodies were making as we peeled away every layer. "I want more babies with you, Augusta Belle." He scraped his teeth along the shell of my ear, hard chest rasping against mine before his fingers stole between us, rough pads spreading my damp flesh. "Want all the babies with you, sunshine."

He pinched my aching flesh, sending a torrent of showers erupting through my body, stars splitting behind my eyelids, before his grip tightened at my waist. He held me close to him, body shaking as his own release pummeled through him.

I felt him flexing deep inside, our bodies softening as he pulled us down into the mountain of cotton that mounded the motel bed.

Violent breaths racked my body as the slow drag of

his cock kissed every raw nerve, the sensation so intense soft pulses shuddered their way through my body. My emotions had already been strung tight the last month, the highs so beautiful, but some days it felt like I was waiting for the inevitable crash.

I snuggled against the only man who'd ever made me feel worthy, but the only thing I wanted was the one thing I couldn't bear to ask because I was too afraid of the answer.

Could we stay?

"The smell of your skin makes my heart happy," I whispered against the soft flesh of his tattooed bicep.

Fallon turned up his lips in something that was part grin, part frown, before he uncurled himself from my body and pushed out of the bed. "You're biased. That means I need a shower." He planted a kiss on the crown of my head.

Sunlight shot through the blinds, highlighting all the finely knit muscles and chiseled contours as he walked away, the padding of his feet on the carpet piercing the silence.

We'd been in Landry for nearly a month, Jack and Calvin welcoming us into their lives without a second's hesitation.

And while things between Fallon and me had been better than ever—fevered late-night writing sessions and lovemaking, waiting for Jack at the bus stop in the afternoons—life had settled into its own rhythm.

But still, this giant, unspoken elephant seemed to exist between us, growing, pushing out the air.

We might have only been here for a month, but already I was thinking the next ten years in Landry looked pretty good, the idea of leaving Jack like a serrated knife working its way down my heart.

But Fallon, as attentive as he was, still seemed like he was missing something.

I didn't know what was on his mind, but he constantly looked like he was in a state of flux, warring with sides of himself I wasn't privy to.

The shower water halted then, and the near-silent sound of his footsteps was the only sign that he was back in the room with me.

I tucked the sheet around my bare body, sliding up to my knees as he neared the bed, white towel secured loosely at his waist, dark licks of ink slashing across the deeply etched muscles of his torso.

I loved him so much, but maybe he was a rolling stone through and through. Maybe he'd always need the road and the crowds to feed a part of himself that I, and Jack, couldn't give.

I swallowed the slow ache that'd lodged in my throat as his hands pushed into the sides of my wild waves before placing quiet kisses on my forehead.

He didn't say anything.

Neither did I.

I didn't know what I could say.

Please don't leave us.

Because, despite everything new we'd found, suddenly my priorities had shifted, *Jack* was now part of my *us*.

The ringing of my phone chose that moment to pierce the haunted silence, and Fallon's hands dropped to his sides before he pulled a clean pair of worn-out jeans from a stack. The phone shook again, and this time, I stretched across the bed, holding it to my ear as I said a quick hello.

I listened silently, sounds of sheer fear lacing the voice on the other line. "Have you seen Jack?"

I swallowed, shaking my head as my heart fell on the floor. "No."

"He left school at lunch and hasn't been back. He's never done this before. The school asked all his friends —" Calvin sounded bad. Scary bad.

My eyes shot across the room to Fallon's, worry transcending the space. "We'll do whatever we can. We can canvass all the neighborhoods from here to the school. Whatever you need from us. We'll find him, Calvin, I promise."

Fallon was pushing his boots onto his feet before I'd hung up the phone.

My stomach turned, the greatest fear I'd ever known materializing in a matter of an instant.

Fallon's eyes searched my face, a frown twisting his features before he crossed the room, wrapping me in his arms and letting me unravel, piece by terrified piece.

"I'll find him, Augusta Belle. Swear on my life, I won't sleep till I find him."

Adrenaline flooded my veins as fat tears streamed down my cheeks. Fallon's thumbs attempted to push the salty tracks aside before I launched off the bed and across the room, throwing on the first pair of jeans I found, wiggling into a bra and then a tank top.

"Maybe you should stay here in case he shows up," Fallon suggested.

I shook my head, rational decision-making no longer a part of my skill set, the holy terror of losing my son, not for the first time, settling into my bones. "I can't just stand by while this…"

I pushed away more tears as I tried to tie my shoelaces.

"Augusta," Fallon murmured, steady palms holding my shaking shoulders. "Take some deep breaths and lift your head up high. We're gonna find him. Post yourself outside, keep your phone turned up, and I'm just gonna do a quick search around the school zone, okay? I'll be back in thirty minutes to check on you, but you've got be ready to take my call, okay? Or if he comes here, just be ready. He needs you, sunshine." Fallon nestled me into his neck. "We all do."

I nodded, summoning my strength as we pushed through the door of the motel room, Fallon giving me one last kiss before he climbed into his truck and backed away.

I swallowed down my tears, grazing my teeth on my bottom lip, and looking down at my phone in my hand.

Without knowing what else to do, I pulled up my contacts, pressing Jack's, the picture of all three of us smiling at the swimming hole a few weeks ago his contact photo.

I cried more happy-sad tears, pressing the speakerphone as the call began to ring. I waited, birds singing sweet songs in the Spanish moss-covered oaks around me, wind carryin' all my hopes away with each passing second.

"'Ello?"

"Jack?" I nearly shrieked, catching the phone in both hands at my face.

"Yeah?" His sweet little twang was like an angel singin' in my heart.

"Where are you!"

He let out a little huff on the line. "Shoulda known Dad would call you."

A hooded figure came around the corner, spiky blond hair and dark brown eyes sending tears of relief down my cheeks. "What, are you crazy?"

I pulled him into a hug, holding him so tightly I

thought I might crush my own chest cavity. I didn't care. I needed to feel him here, safe.

"You scared us."

He nodded, pushing the hood off his head and dropping his backpack on the sidewalk before he plopped onto the nearest picnic table. "I just needed a break."

"A break?" I sat down beside him. "I get that, buddy, but you've just got to tell people first."

He swallowed, his eyes avoiding mine as he twisted his hands together.

"What's on your mind? Did something happen today?"

He shook his head, troubled eyes conveying more than he was willing to say out loud.

"I'm gonna send your dad and Fallon a quick message, and then I want to know exactly what's going on in that head of yours."

"What if you're mad?"

"I won't be mad, Jack. Not ever. I might be worried, but I promise you that anger isn't something you'll get as long as you tell me the truth."

He nodded again, breathing a reluctant sigh when I hit send on the two messages confirming Jack's whereabouts.

"I'm just worried that I'm gonna get home from school someday and you won't be here."

His words hollowed out my soul, the sheer worry in his innocent little eyes leveling me. "That won't happen, Jack."

My voice was barely above a whisper, my promise to him as much as myself.

"But Fallon's got his music. I know he doesn't want a kid—"

"You don't know what Fallon wants at all, Jack. And the best part, you don't even have to worry about it. Fallon and I will work out all those adult things."

The man of the hour pulled in then, bright white truck parking alongside us.

Fallon Gentry unfolded his big body from behind the wheel of his truck, a look of relief dominating every feature of his face.

He smiled, taking long strides to Jack and then placing a kiss on his head before wrapping me in a quick hug. "Scared the hell outta us for a minute, kid."

Jack smiled weakly when Fallon plopped down beside him, crossing one ankle over a knee and cocking his arms back on the bench.

The way he filled up a space did things, swallowed up the energy around him. Drew people into his bubble like moths to a flame. It was exactly the thing the crowd witnessed all those nights he sat onstage, exactly why he'd made it so far in Nashville, and why he would have made it much further if he'd chosen that life.

But the longer he seemed to stew on what he wanted to do next, the more he seemed to be unhappy about it.

"I know someday you're going to go back on the road," Jack's meek little voice finally admitted.

Fallon rubbed a hand through his beard, body still easy, casual. "Ever heard that sayin' 'bout assumin' things?"

Jack tilted his head, shaking it finally in confusion.

Fallon nodded. "Well, when you go assumin' things, Jack—"

"I think he's a little on the young side for this particular lesson," I interjected, hand on Jack's shoulder.

"What's assumin'?" Jack scrunched up his cute little button nose, and I couldn't help laughing.

"It means you're wrong if you think I'm leavin' anytime soon." Fallon wrapped an arm around him. "Couldn't get rid of me if you wanted to."

Jack's grin split his face, Fallon's hand in his hair, messing up the cute little style he'd been rocking.

"But how're you gonna make music?" Concern etched Jack's small features, showing he'd put a lot of time into thinking about just this.

"It's a new world, little man. Gotta lotta different options, and all of 'em involve me 'n' Augusta livin' right here next to you."

Jack's grin grew even wider, and he jumped up on the picnic table, cheering before Fallon stood and gave him double high fives.

"But you can't go pullin' stuff like this again. Scared your dad and us real bad, Jack."

Jack leaped from the table, still smiling. "Promise I won't."

"Good." Fallon slid an arm over his shoulders and pulled him in close for a hug. "Your dad asked me to bring you back to school. That sound okay, or is there anythin' else that needs addressin'?"

Jack shook his head, beaming smile still etching his lips before he spun, running across the sidewalk to launch himself into my arms. I held him close, breathing in the fresh sunshine and sweet, sweet honey scent of his hair, more grateful for both the men in my life than I'd ever been.

Fallon's warm embrace encompassed both of us, his lips brushing against my forehead. "Been thinkin' maybe it's time we settled down and bought a house. Thought in the morning maybe we could visit a few Realtors?"

I shot my eyes to his, speechless, and nodding. "Yes!"

He laughed, looping me in for a hug. "Well, at least I got one enthusiastic yes out of you."

"Are you sure you're ready? Weren't you just sayin' you weren't the settlin' type?"

He shrugged, pushing one hand into his beard as he thought. "That was then. Game's changed now."

"So it has," I mused, sitting up a little straighter.

I had hope.

I had my boys.

There would be no taking either one of them away from me again.

If it meant becomin' a permanent resident of Landry, then roll out the welcome wagon. I'd be a proud, flag-totin' citizen of the great state of Mississippi. As long as I had these boys, my life would be complete.

My future, since the very first time I'd had Fallon, felt so bright.

EPILOGUE

Augusta - three months later

"Boys!" I called down the stairs, voice lost among the clatter of noise coming out of the basement studio. "Dinner!" I grinned when the sound system finally switched off, laughter floating up the stairs to greet my happy ears.

After two weeks of searching, a cash bid, and a horrendous few days in a moving truck driving all the way from Tennessee down to Mississippi, we were finally settled in Landry. Our house was just a half a mile from Jack Christopher's, near enough to ride a bike to, and almost near enough to throw a baseball at. I knew— Fallon and Jack had tried, making it their new challenge to launch a baseball with a potato gun from his backyard to ours.

We were that close.

We were that happy.

Things were that good.

"Learned the opening lines of 'Hotel California' today!" Jack buzzed into the kitchen, gleeful grin on his face.

He was barefoot, both boys were as they entered the kitchen, so at home and cozy in the not-so-little house Fallon had bought.

Apparently, he hadn't been kidding when he said he wanted to settle.

I was thinking maybe we'd rent a while first, but Fallon had plans far beyond my wildest dreams.

His first order of business was outfitting a basement bedroom into a home music studio, recording equipment and mixers to his heart's content.

Once in a while when I woke up to find the bed empty beside me, I found him down there, mixing new songs or working on lyrics. Watching Fallon make music was a dream come true, like watching magic unfold before my eyes. He inspired me to spend more time writing, some of my lyrics even finding their way into his songs.

He'd already been more active on his once-defunct video channel, the one that'd first launched his career. And while TMZ hadn't caught up with us yet, the buzz around where Fallon Gentry was producing his music, and the new, modern sound he was creating—a catchy blend of Southern rock and bluesy-country—already had the channel growing exponentially. It only took one new remix of "Whiskey Girl," a duet where we shared the haunting lyrics of his hit song, to go viral, and attention grew. And then the largest streaming channel came callin', offerin' a one-night unplugged performance featuring Fallon that they wanted to film and release to the masses. Fallon had the chance to go worldwide again.

And after so many sleepless nights of considering all the possibilities, we finally said yes.

Fallon insisted that we sing "Whiskey Girl" together, and even asked if I'd perform a few of my own songs alongside him, along with his other crowd favorites. He went from being a Nashville has-been to building his own career from the ground up, exactly how he wanted it.

He inspired me more every day.

His sister was glad he was finally settled, her updating of his fly-by-night tour schedule on the website not needed anymore because he was no longer doing public gigs. And I could update the website now if required anyway.

But the true gift, the one that put all else to shame, was watching him be a dad to Jack.

Calvin had been generous, allowing Jack to move back and forth between our homes from day one.

Jack had now taken to callin' me Mom, which slayed

my heart with so many happy tears I'd nearly broken down in front of the poor kid, and Fallon Pa, which made me laugh more every time he said it.

And the way Fallon's eyes crinkled at the corners made me think he liked it too.

It took weeks for us to truly settle into our new roles as parents, being good role models and watching our words, adapting to the idea that something made up of equal parts of us walked around outside of our bodies every day.

I 'didn't think either of us had ever felt so vulnerable, so responsible, and so overwhelmed with love to get the chance.

We also had to make peace with the time we'd lost with our sweet boy, Fallon taking an especially long time to adjust. But the more he lost himself in the music, the more his true feelings seemed to come out in the lyrics.

Staying busy and creating what he loved was therapy, more than whiskey ever had been, and he was finally in a good enough place to see the light.

After dinner, once we'd walked Jack home and we were both wandering the hallways of our all-too-often empty house, Fallon caught up with me, wrapping me in his arms from behind and guiding me out into the silver moonlight of our back porch.

I looked up across the fields and forests that surrounded our little neighborhood, and knowing the same moon cast light a few houses down on our son, tucked in and well-loved, I felt truly at peace.

I wasn't running, I wasn't chasing, I wasn't even searching for Fallon. I could finally stop, pause, enjoy, and just be.

"I think it's time we expand this little family we've built," he whispered at my ear, sending a pleasurable chill running down my spine.

I turned up my lips, my hands holding his and bringing them to my belly. "We already have, Gentry."

His muscles stiffened, arms spinning me to assess my face head on. "Does that mean what I think it means?"

I nodded, warm tears pooling at my eyelashes as I thought of all the love we had to give, how great a brother Jack would be, the life we'd build in Landry, makin' music and bein' free. Finally free of the past, of anyone else's expectations, of everything.

"I was thinkin' the name Jett." I pressed a kiss to his inked knuckle. "Or Presley."

Happiness shot through Fallon as he hoisted me in his arms, spinning me in circles while still managing to hold me gently.

"I don't give a shit what we call it. You just made me the happiest man alive, Augusta Belle."

I giggled, his beard tickling across the hot skin at my chest.

That beard had gotten me in trouble all those weeks

ago.

I just couldn't say no to him. His overprotective nature was so attuned to me, the way his hand hovered at my waist as we stood in line, how he pulled out my chair when we sat down for dinner, how he tucked me into bed with such care each night, as if he wanted to memorize every moment we had together.

Fallon, from the moment we'd met, had never stopped making me feel special.

"Swear, Augusta Belle, still surprisin' me." He shook his head, catching my lips with his.

I moaned, hands working at the nape of his neck as sparks of desire ran through my veins.

"I think this is the part where you finally say yes to that question I've been askin'."

"Oh?" I breathed, too caught up in him to even think straight.

"You know." He was working his hand between my legs, coaxing the answer he wanted out of me.

"Sure I don't have any more secrets up my sleeve?" I half teased.

"Don't care." The roughened pad of his thumb slid between my breasts, yanking down the neckline of my dress as he went.

"Are you sure? There was just one more thing…"

"Really don't care, Augusta Belle." He caught my lips in a kiss meant to hush me. "Nothin' you could say could make me change my mind. Been to hell and back with you already, Mama. Might as well make this official."

I hummed, expressing quiet reservation. "Nothing at all?"

He huffed, finally growing exasperated with my line of questioning. "You could tell me you've got triplets in there, and I'd be a happy fucker. What could you possibly have on your mind that needs sayin' at this minute?" He slid a palm against the small of my back and applied pressure, our hips grinding together as he showed me exactly what I did to him.

"Well, the more we've talked to Calvin, it's just gotten me thinkin' 'bout that day, Fallon. And somethin' 'bout it doesn't sit right."

"Oh yeah?" He sighed out a breath at my ear, still not paying attention.

"So I got to diggin' through that box—"

"Shit, diggin' up the past again?" He finally stilled, hands at my shoulders and eyes on me. "What'd you find this time?"

"Nothin' much really." I thought back to the stack of papers I'd found just this morning when the boys were still asleep. "Just a background check, but it was on your dad. And dated the day…well, *that* day. I'm assumin' my dad did it at work, but it had your address on it, and it just got me thinkin'. What if he… Well, your dad believed it was arson, right?"

Fallon nodded, eyes shuttering closed before he pushed a hand through his hair. "Yup."

"What made him think that?" I asked, still piecing everything together.

Fallon whipped his eyes up to meet mine, a strangled look covering his face. "Because I saw someone."

"*You* saw someone? The person your dad thinks started the fire?"

Fallon nodded, eyes searching the ground at his feet. "Person throwin' a gasoline-soaked rag in a bottle."

My eyes popped wide, heart throttling to a gallop as I realized there was more about that night Fallon hadn't told me. "Who did you see?"

He worked his hand back and forth at his beard, eyes closed as he tilted his head up almost in slow motion. "Didn't get a real good look." His throat looked tight as he swallowed. "But they were drivin' a green Volvo."

My heart slammed to a halt, unable to form the words I knew I needed.

His eyes avoided mine, his hands rubbing at his face and head, anything to take his mind off the conversation.

"Really?" I finally squealed, tears welling. "You're sure?"

Fallon's eyes finally hung heavy on mine, the same dark irises that'd pulled me in so long ago, made my heart sing and were the only thing that made life worth livin' for so long. "Sure enough that I couldn't bring myself to tell you."

"No." I dropped into his arms, covering his T-shirt in my tears as I thought about all the lies, all the regrets, all the awful things my father had done and hidden from me. He'd taken so many secrets to his grave and left them all for me to uncover. Peeling them away one layer at a time.

Fallon stroked my arms, doing his best to soothe me. My father's decision to put Fallon in his will suddenly made sense. He'd taken Fallon's home from him, I guessed in some small way he thought he could give it back.

I just wished he would have been around to explain it all. Living without the closure of what really happened had brought about a slow death for all of us.

"That's how I know we can get through anything, Augusta Belle. Because we already have," he finally crooned, pulling me into his lap as he settled us down into the porch couch cushions. "You know what that old-timer said. I act too damn old for my age." His playful smile did its job and began healing me little by little. "The upside of that is when I know somethin's right. I know this is right, and you and I are right as rain together, Augusta Belle. Whiskey and sunshine, soft angles and rough edges. Nothin' about us has ever made sense, and that's exactly the reason we make perfect sense."

I swallowed the lump still lingering in my throat, ready to leave the past where it belonged and move on with the only man who had ever made me feel like me.

"Yes."

"Say again?" He tilted his head to the side, cocky grin lifting up his lips.

"Yes, Fallon Gentry. I'll be your wife. As long as you promise me we'll keep makin' music together, I'm in."

That mischievous grin that'd stolen my heart from the start deepened. "So long as you promise me we can keep makin' babies together…"

I swiped at his shoulder, but his reflexes were too quick, and he caught my wrist in his hand, turned it over, and slipped a canary diamond the size of the state of Mississippi onto my finger. His lips hovered over mine, eyes crinkling with unbridled joy.

"Here's to music, babies, love, and my whiskey girl."

THE END

Sign-up for new release alerts from me and get the Whiskey Girl extended epilogue and playlist!
https://www.subscribepage.com/WhiskeyGirl

COMING OCTOBER 2018

REBEL SAINT

She walked into his church wounded and seeking solace. What she didn't expect to find was temptation so sharp and sweet under one snow-white collar.

Their relationship was never innocent.

From the beginning, their attraction was combustible, the magnetism all-consuming, every touch wrought with explosive tension, begging them to succumb to their darkest desire…

Eve was Adam's first taste of the forbidden fruit. Father Rafe and Tressa give forbidden a whole new meaning.

ADD Rebel Saint to Goodreads!
New release alert sign-up: https://
www.subscribepage.com/WhiskeyGirl
Bloggers! Help me share *Rebel Saint!* *https://goo.gl/
forms/zguPouf6E4RqhO0C2*
Check out my website *www.adrianeleigh.com* to
learn more!

MORE FROM ADRIANE

*For those new to her work, consider the USA Today bestseller **Wild**, **Sweet Alibi**, or the following standalones:*

★ Experience edgy glamour and forbidden love in the fast-paced erotic suspense <u>BLINDSIGHT</u>.

★ Fall in love with a spellbinding student-teacher romance about love that overcomes all odds in <u>BEAUTIFUL BURN</u>.

★ Get carried away with sexy, enigmatic billionaire Carter Morgan in the Amazon Top 20 bestseller <u>STEEL and LACE</u>.

"Sexy. Hot. Leigh leaves you wanting more!" - **K. Bromberg, Driven**

"Sizzling chemistry, a glamorous world, plot twists…a perfect combination held together with Adriane Leigh's addictive writing. I dove into this world, and didn't want to come up for air. I can't wait for more!" - **Alessandra Torre, Hollywood Dirt**

"Adriane Leigh never dissapoints with equal amounts of heat and heart with all the sex, suspense and scandal…Leigh's newest mysterious hero will have you anxiously flipping pages well into the night trying to uncover his secrets." - **Jay Crownover, Marked Men**

* * *

Don't miss a release! Sign up for the newsletter to find out about new releases and sales: **http://www.adrianeleigh.com/contact**

Follow her on Facebook, Twitter (@AdrianeLeigh), or Instagram (@adriane.leigh.writer).